Gustav Me

Walpurgisnacht

Translated by Mike Mitchell
and with an introduction
by Ingrid O. Fischer

Dedalus

Published in the UK by Dedalus Limited,
24-26, St Judith's Lane, Sawtry, Cambs, PE28 5XE
Email: info@ dedalusbooks.com
www.dedalusbooks.com

ISBN   978 1 907650 17 8

Dedalus is distributed in the USA and Canada by SCB Distributors,
15608 South New Century Drive, Gardena, CA 90248
email: info@scbdistributors.com   web: www.scbdistributors.com

Dedalus is distributed in Australia by Peribo Pty Ltd.
58, Beaumont Road, Mount Kuring-gai, N.S.W. 2080
email: info@peribo.com.au

Publishing History
First published in Germany in 1917
First published by Dedalus in 1993
New edition in 2011

Translation © copyright Mike Mitchell and Dedalus 1993
Introduction © copyright Ingrid O.Fischer and Dedalus

The right of Mike Mitchell to be identified as the translator of this work has
been asserted by him in accordance with the Copyright, Design and Patent Act,
1988

Printed in Finland by Bookwell
Typeset by Refine Catch Ltd, Bungay, Suffolk

A C.I.P. listing for this book is available on request.

THE TRANSLATOR

For many years an academic with a special interest in Austrian literature and culture, Mike Mitchell has been a freelance literary translator since 1995. He is one of Dedalus's editorial directors and is responsible for the Dedalus translation programme.

He has published over fifty translations from German and French, including Gustav Meyrink's five novels and *The Dedalus Book of Austrian Fantasy*. His translation of Rosendorfer's *Letters Back to Ancient China* won the 1998 Schlegel-Tieck Translation Prize after he had been shortlisted in previous years for his translations of *Stephanie* by Herbert Rosendorfer and *The Golem* by Gustav Meyrink.

His translations have been shortlisted three times for The Oxford Weidenfeld Translation Prize: *Simplicissimus* by Johann Grimmelshausen in 1999, *The Other Side* by Alfred Kubin in 2000 and *The Bells of Bruges* by Georges Rodenbach in 2008.

His biography of Gustav Meyrink:*Vivo:The Life of Gustav Meyrink* was published by Dedalus in November 2008. He has recently edited and translated *The Dedalus Meyrink Reader*.

Books by and about Gustav Meyrink which are available from Dedalus:

The five novels translated by Mike Mitchell:

The Golem
The Angel of the West Window
The Green Face
Walpurgisnacht
The White Dominican

A collection of short stories translated by Maurice Raraty:

The Opal (and other stories)

A sampler for Gustav Meyrink's complete works edited and translated by Mike Mitchell:

The Dedalus Meyrink Reader

The first English language biography of Gustav Meyrink written by Mike Mitchell:

Vivo: The Life of Gustav Meyrink

INTRODUCTION TO *WALPURGISNACHT*

When *Walpurgisnacht* was published in 1917, the world was
enmeshed in the First World War which led to the final destruction of the Austro-Hungarian monarchy.

The Austro-Hungarian monarchy was a multinational state,
her people spoke German, Hungarian, Italian and half a dozen
Slavonic languages. The only bond of union was in the person
of the aged emperor, and only the officers of the army and the
higher civil servants felt any great loyalty to him. The kind of
feudal political organization the Emperor represented had been
out of date since the French Revolution. By 1914 Austria-
Hungary had been spiritually dead for 125 years. There was of
course plenty of patriotic feeling within the Empire: German
nationalism, Italian, Rumanian and Serbian nationalism, each
eager to extend its own frontiers. In addition there was Hungarian, Czech, Slovak and Polish nationalism, but very little feeling for the Austro-Hungarian empire as such.

The assassination of Archduke Ferdinand and his wife
Sophie in Sarajevo in June 1914 was simply the spark that lit the
fire which would make this European trouble-spot boil over.

In 1917 the Russian revolution broke out. The German and
Austrian empires were heartened by the collapse of Russia, but
still in October 1917 the break-up of the Austro-Hungarian
army began, and the rulers in Vienna sued for an armistice.

By the time *Walpurgisnacht* was published, Gustav Meyrink
had long left Prague, the city he loved and hated the most. He
was living in a house called "the house at the last lamp" at Lake
Starnberg in Bavaria, the house where he was to die in 1932.

Since *Walpurgisnacht* is the only novel, apart from *The
Green Face*, in which Meyrink used current events, it is important to understand the European situation in which it was written.
Walpurgisnacht is situated in Prague during the First World
War. Prague was the town Meyrink drew most of his creative
and spiritual inspiration from, it was a place he deeply loved and
just as deeply hated. Since he was born the bastard son of an

actress and an aristocratic German diplomat, the snobbish society of Prague shunned him and never regarded him as an equal. On the other hand his flamboyant and eccentric appearance aroused envy and dislike among those he wanted to be his peers. His first marriage was a complete failure, and when Meyrink met Philomena Bernt, his future second wife, he encountered strong opposition, especially from her brother. Prague's high society took exception to this elegant, mysterious half-aristocrat and he became embroiled in scandals, which brought him to the brink of social and economic ruin. Meyrink, who never did things by half measure, once challenged the whole corps of army officers to a duel. On the pretext of his illegitimacy, they declared him "not qualified to give satisfaction", thereby emphasizing his second-rate status as a human being.

In 1904 Meyrink, completely disheartened by the treatment he encountered from society, left Prague for good. After a short period in Vienna and travelling, he found his permanent home in Bavaria at Lake Starnberg where he spent many happy years with his second wife and children. Although Meyrink never went back to Prague, it remained the creative inspiration for his work. Its unique atmosphere, its mysterious, dark and haunting presence never ceased to influence his personal development and work. Meyrink may have been comfortable in "the house at the last lamp", but Prague remained his spiritual home. All the battles he fought there were the same battles he had to fight inside himself. In all his works we find them taking place on two levels: on the immanent-rational level and on the transcendental-irrational, where conflicts are resolved in dimensions beyond the earthly. Hermann Beckh, a fellow writer and thinker, said about Meyrink: "He echoed with the highest human and eternal problems, he looked into the depths of humanity and the soul, he looked into his own fate".

What was merely hinted at in *The Green Face*, namely the inevitable and necessary destruction of the world, is spelled out painfully and clearly in *Walpurgisnacht*. Nothing in this world is complete, and there is no salvation in it.

"Walpurgisnacht", the night of the 30th April, has always been considered a time of evil. During the witch hunts of an earlier age Walpurgisnacht was considered most dangerous for a "good Christian soul": it was a pagan feast of the flesh, a feast of carnal desires! It was celebrated (and still is) to ensure the fertility of the land and its people for the coming year. Fires were lit to celebrate the re-awakening of fertility and life, and one leaped over the fire to win the lover one desired. The horned god Pan presided in sensuality and joy of life as god and goddess were united in an orgiastic embrace. Wild and unfettered sexuality was unleashed to ensure the fertility of the land and its people in the year to come. It is a day which marks a change – from the dark and barren days of winter to the light and promising days of spring. A change, a rejection of old values in the hope of a new beginning, with all the uncertainty that implies.

In our novel Walpurgisnacht starts with a whist party. The people involved are perfect caricatures of the "trottelig" or fossilized aristocratic society, which had long outlived its day and purpose. Meyrink is a masterful depictor of human weakness and of the folly of strutting self-importance and ignorance of the real world. Yet, out of all of them, one figure catches the reader's eye: Dr. Thaddaeus Halberd, former physician to the Imperial Court, last in a long line of doctors who were true aristocrats, not so much by accident of birth as by deeds. His nickname "Penguin" reveals the boundaries imposed on him by birth. A penguin cannot fly, but it can waddle, and things therefore take a little longer ...

On the first pages of the first chapter we are introduced to Zrcadlo (the mirror), who has the uncanny ability to become the image of whatever person is present and needing to be taught a lesson or shown their darker side – or so it seems at first. Some pages on we meet Polyxena, the niece of old Countess Zahradka and of Baron Elsenwanger. Her male counterpart appears in the figure of Ottokar Vondrejc, the violin student at the conservatoire. All the other figures in the novel, apart from Lizzie the

9

Czech, provide little more than background scenery.

As with *The Golem* and *The Green Face*, we have a handful of protagonists, who carry all the action. As in most of Meyrink's works, there is a young couple whose relationship will lead to a higher spiritual union or "chymical marriage". Then there is a solitary old man, seemingly without connection with the young couple yet profoundly influencing their development. In *Walpurgisnacht*, we find the additional figure of Zrcadlo, the mirror, who drives the action on as a kind of devil's advocate. From his first appearance, when he unveils the hypocrisy of the old coward, Baron Elsenwanger, he reveals to Halberd the emptiness and aimlessness of his life. He also alters the course of history by bringing back the figure of the legendary Jan Žižka of Trocnov, the revolutionary and radical Hussite. This novel seems to require such an *agent provocateur*, because its leading figures are either too weak to force the action along or too frightened of change in their personal lives. Zrcadlo forces them to face their mirror image and alter their ways, even to the extent of having their lives destroyed.

Meyrink emphasizes that our body is merely a shell, inhabited by our true self, the "I" which is the essence of our being, the driving force which makes us return life after life to learn and perfect ourselves: "the self is the master". Later we read: "The highest wisdom appears dressed as a clown .... Once we have recognised something as 'dress', once we have seen through it, then it can only be a clown's costume, and anyone who is in possession of his 'self' sees his own body – and those of others – as merely a clown's costume." Still, our body is the only material agent by which our "self" is able to make its mark upon the world – and the essence of this body is our blood. Blood is life, blood is sensuality as opposed to the fossilized senility of the aristocrats. Through blood we can find our "self", through blood we are one with our ancestors, we experience their sense of life and can unite with their will and forge a new understanding.

When *Walpurgisnacht* was first published there was a

rumour that Meyrink had been asked to write a novel which suggested that the Freemasons were responsible for the outbreak of the First World War. Meyrink was not prepared to do this. His answer to this despicable offer can be found in one paragraph, where he states that in masonic rituals one has to take a step backwards in order to become a master. All the protagonists in "Walpurgisnacht" do it. Polyxena encounters an ancestor who, having poisoned her husband, went mad imprisoned in the grey dungeon of the Dalibor Tower. She relives all of her great-grandmother's wildness, her unbounded sexuality, but fails in the end to take the true step backwards which could possibly have saved the world. Instead, she pulls the bell of Sacré Coeur and decides, "That is where I want my picture to hang".

Ottokar Vondrejc, the adopted son of the veteran soldier and housekeeper of the Dalibor Tower, knows in his heart that his true ancestors are of royal blood and allows himself to be crowned the Emperor of the new aeon. His weak physical constitution and his determination to prove his love to Polyxena let him down in the end. All that remains is a lifeless caricature of an emperor as dead as the Empire itself.

The only figure to master his past and take a step forward is Dr. Thaddaeus Halberd. He realizes that upholding the tradition of his ancestral lineage of doctors is not enough to qualify him as a worthwhile human being. Lizzie the Czech with her devoted love for Halberd opens for him the door to a higher understanding of the purpose of life, and thus, although it is never consummated, the true chymical marriage is theirs. "His eyes were fixed on the point in the distance where the rails met. 'The place where they meet is eternity', he muttered to himself, 'that is the place where everything will be transformed.' " His death stands for the death of a way of life: the end of false and outdated values. Sometimes it is necessary to destroy old values to make way for a new beginning.

Meyrink's *Walpurgisnacht* does just that. It is his way of saying goodbye to Prague and the old world, and welcoming the chance of a new beginning. When Ottokar in his final struggle to prove to Polyxena that he is worthy of her love, shouts out to Countess Zahradka, "Mother, mother!", she shoots him through the forehead but cannot prevent the course of history. This shows that Meyrink finally managed to "kill his mother" (as the English occultist Aleister Crowley insisted, this is the first step on the path to becoming a true magician), killing Prague and with it all the outworn values.

The chymical marriage Meyrink tries to achieve in all his novels was experienced in his personal life with his second wife Philomena. Many critics have dismissed him as no more than a cynic and satirist, but I think he finally proved otherwise: "He was a living man. Both here and beyond."

Ingrid O. Fisher

Walpurgisnacht

Chapter One

Zrcadlo the Actor

A dog barked.

Once. A second time.

Then a noiseless hush, as if in the darkness the animal were pricking up its ears for any suspicious sounds.

"I think that was Brock barking", said old Baron Elsenwanger. "That will probably be Schirnding coming."

"Lord help us, that's no reason for barking", objected Countess Zahradka, an old woman with snow-white ringlets, a sharp Roman nose and bushy brows over her large, black, crazed eyes; she seemed irritated at Brock's unseemly behaviour, and shuffled the pack of cards even faster than she had been doing for the last half hour already.

"What does he actually do, all day long?" asked Dr. Thaddaeus Halberd. With his clean-shaven, intelligent, wrinkled face above an old-fashioned lace cravat, the former Physician to the Imperial Court looked like the spectre of one of his own ancestors; he was sitting opposite the Countess, curled up in a wing chair, his incredibly long, skinny legs drawn up ape-like almost to his chin.

The students on the Hradschin called him the 'Penguin', and they would laugh at him when, every day on the dot of twelve outside the Castle courtyard, he would climb into a closed cab, the roof of which had to be laboriously raised and then lowered again before he could fit all of his six foot six into it. The process of disembarkation was just as complicated when the cab stopped, a few hundred yards further on, outside Schnell's, where Halberd used to peck at his luncheon with jerky, bird-like movements.

"Who would you be referring to?" asked Baron Elsenwanger, "Brock or Schirnding?"

"*Whom*", the Penguin corrected him.

"To – who – would – you – be – referring", interrupted the Countess reprovingly, emphasising every word. The two old gentlemen fell into an embarrassed silence.

Again the dog out in the garden barked, a deep bark this time, almost a howl.

Immediately the dark, curved mahogany door decorated with a pastoral scene opened and His Excellency, Privy Counsellor Baron Caspar von Schirnding entered, wearing, as usual when he came to a whist evening in Elsenwanger House, tight black trousers with his slightly chubby figure enveloped in an old-fashioned russet frock-coat made of marvellously soft cloth.

Without a word, he scurried across to a chair, deposited his straight-brimmed top hat on the floor underneath it and then ceremonially kissed the Countess' hand.

"And why would he still be barking", muttered the Penguin pensively.

"This time he means Brock", Countess Zahradka explained, with a preoccupied glance at Baron Elsenwanger.

"But you're covered in perspiration, Counsellor. We can't have you catching cold", the latter exclaimed, paused, then suddenly started to squawk, with an operatic trill, into the darkness of the adjoining room, that immediately lit up as if by magic, "Božena, Božena, Bo-shaaaynah, would you serve the supper, please – prosím."

The company went into the dining room and sat round the large table.

Only the Penguin stalked stiffly along the walls, marvelling at the scenes from the battle between David and Goliath on the tapestries, as if seeing them for the first time, and running a connoisseur's hand along the magnificent curves of the Maria Theresa chairs.

"I've been down there! In the world!" exclaimed von Schirnding, mopping his brow with an enormous, red and yellow checked handkerchief. "And I took the opportunity to have my hair cut." He ran his finger round the inside of his collar, as if his neck were itchy.

Four times a year he would make such remarks, suggesting that desperate measures were needed to keep his hair under control, deluding himself that nobody knew he wore wigs, first short-cropped ones and then others with longer locks. His quarterly comments were always received with murmurs of astonishment, but this time his companions were so astounded when they heard *where* he had been that they forgot their traditional exclamations.

"What? Down there? In the world? In Prague? You?" Dr. Halberd whirled round in amazement. "You?"

The other two were open-mouthed. "In the world! Down there! In Prague!"

Finally the Countess managed to stutter, "But – but then you must have gone over the bridge! What if it had collapsed?!"

"Collapsed!! Lord preserve us!" croaked Baron Elsenwanger, and went pale. "Touch wood." He went over to the stove where there was still a log left from the winter, picked it up, spat on it three times and threw it into the empty fireplace. "Touch wood!"

Božena, the maid, dressed in a ragged smock and headscarf – and barefoot, as was still the custom in old-fashioned aristocratic households in Prague – brought in a magnificent tureen of heavy, beaten silver.

"Aaah! Sausage soup!" Countess Zahradka gave a satisfied growl and dropped her lorgnette: the maid's fingers, in white kid gloves that were much too large, were submerged in the soup and the Countess had taken them for sausages.

"I took ... the electric tram!" von Schirnding gasped, still mindful of his great adventure.

The others exchanged glances: they were beginning to doubt his words. Only the Penguin maintained a stony expression.

"The last time I was down there – in Prague – was thirty years ago!" groaned Baron Elsenwanger, shaking his head as he tied his napkin round his neck. The ends stuck out behind his ears, making him look like a large, timid white rabbit. "For my poor brother's funeral in the Týn Church."

"In my whole life I've never been to Prague at all", declared the Countess with a shudder. "Catch me going there! When they executed my ancestors in the Old Town Square!"

"Well, yes, but that was back in the Thirty Years War, dear Countess", said the Penguin, in an attempt to calm her down. "It was a long time ago."

"Fiddlesticks; it seems like yesterday to me. Damned Prussians, the lot of 'em." The Countess stared absent-mindedly at her soup, puzzled to find no sausages in it; then she shot a glance through her lorgnette across the table, to see if one of the gentlemen there might have sneaked them from her.

For a moment she was deep in thought and muttered to herself, "Blood, blood, how it spurts out when someone's head is chopped off." Then, turning to von Schirnding, she said aloud, "Were you not frightened, Counsellor? What if you had fallen into the hands of the Prussians, down there in Prague?"

"The Prussians? We're hand in hand with the Prussians now."

"Are we now? So the war's finally over? I'm not surprised; I expect Windischgrätz gave them a good thrashing again."

"No, Countess", said the Penguin. "For three years now we have been allied to the Prussians" ("Al-lied!" confirmed Elsenwanger emphatically) "with whom – I mean, with *who* – we are fighting shoulder to shoulder against the Russians. It is – " He broke off politely when he noticed the Countess' ironic, incredulous smile.

The conversation came to a stop, and for half an hour all that could be heard was the scraping of knives and spoons or the soft slap of Božena's bare feet as she went round the table serving new dishes.

Baron Elsenwanger wiped his lips. "Well Countess, gentlemen, I think it's time we – "

A low, long-drawn-out howl from the garden sounded through the summer night and cut him short.

"Jesusandmary, an omen! Death is in the house!"

18

When the Penguin had pulled aside the heavy satin curtains and opened the glass door behind them that led onto the balcony they could hear one of the servants down in the park cursing the dog in a low voice, "Quiet Brock, you blasted mangy cur!"

A flood of moonlight poured into the room and the flames of the candles in the crystal chandeliers flickered and smouldered in the soft breeze redolent with acacias. Far below, on the other side of the Moldau, Prague was slumbering beneath a sea of mist, from which a reddish haze rose up towards the stars. Against this background, a man was walking, slowly and very upright, along the barely three-inch-wide parapet of the high park wall. He had his hands stretched out in front of him like a blind man; at times he would be half swallowed up by the sharp silhouettes of the branches of the trees, as if the glittering moonlight had suddenly curdled, at others he was vividly illuminated, as if he were floating over the blackness.

Dr. Halberd could not believe his eyes. For a moment he thought he must be dreaming, until the sudden, furious barking of the dog brought him down to earth again; he heard a piercing scream, saw the figure on the parapet wobble and then, as if swept away by a silent gust of wind, disappear.

The rustling of bushes and the crack of breaking branches told him that the man had fallen into the garden.

"Thief! Murder! Fetch the police!" shrieked Counsellor von Schirnding, who, together with the Countess, had jumped up and run to the door when they heard the scream. Konstantin Elsenwanger had fallen gibbering to his knees, burying his face in the cushions of his armchair, and was repeating the Lord's Prayer, his hands together and still clutching a leg of roast chicken.

The Penguin rushed onto the balcony and, like some gigantic night-bird with featherless wing-stumps, was gesticulating from the balustrade down into the darkness, where the servants from the porter's lodge, urged on by his shrill commands, had run out into the park with lanterns and were searching the dark groves amid a welter of shouts and curses. The dog seemed to have trapped the intruder, to judge by the loud barks that came at regular intervals.

"Well then, what is it? Have you finally managed to catch the Prussian cossack?" fumed the Countess, who from the very beginning had not shown the least trace of excitement or fear, leaning out of the open window.

"Holy Mother of God, he's broken his neck!" they heard Božena wail; then the men carried a lifeless body from the foot of the wall into the light falling from the dining room onto the lawn.

"Bring him up here. Quickly, before he bleeds to death", ordered the Countess in her calm, icy voice, ignoring the whimpering of her host, who made horrified protest and suggested they should throw the dead man over the wall and down the slope before he could come back to life again.

"At least take him into the picture gallery", pleaded Elsenwanger, pushing the old lady and the Penguin, who had picked up one of the candelabras, into the room full of portraits of his ancestors, and locking the door behind them.

Apart from a table and a few carved chairs with high, gilt arms, there was no furniture in the elongated room, which was more of a corridor. From the musty smell of decay and the layer of dust it was obvious that it was never aired and that it was a long time since anyone had been there.

The life-size pictures were not in frames but let into the panelling. There were portraits of men in leather jerkins, parchment scrolls held imperiously in their hands; women with high lace collars and puffed sleeves; a knight in a white cloak bearing the Maltese cross; a young, ash-blonde lady in a crinoline, beauty spots on cheek and chin, her depraved features exhibiting a cruel, lasciviously sweet smile, with wonderful hands, a thin, straight nose, delicately chiselled nostrils and slender, high-arched brows over her greenish-blue eyes; a nun in the habit of the Barnabites; a page; a cardinal with lean, ascetic fingers, lead-grey lids and a meditative, colourless expression. Each stood in a niche, so that it looked as if they were coming into the room out of dark passageways, woken from centuries of sleep by the flickering gleam of the candles and the unrest in the house. At times they seemed to be stealthily leaning forward, taking care that their clothes should not rustle and betray them, at others to be moving their lips, twitching their fingers or raising their brows, to freeze immediately, as if they were holding their breath and stopping their hearts from beating, whenever either of the two living people happened to glance at them.

"You'll not be able to save him, Halberd", said the Countess, her gaze fixed on the door. "It will be just the same as all those years ago. You remember. He'll have a dagger in his heart. Again you'll say 'He's beyond all human aid, I'm afraid'."

For a moment the former Court Doctor had no idea what she was referring to. Then he suddenly understood. He had come across it before: she used sometimes to mix up the past and the present. The scene from the past that was confusing her suddenly came to life within him. Many, many years ago, in her palace on the Hradschin, her son, who had been stabbed, had been carried into a room. And it had been preceded by a cry from the garden and a dog barking, just the same as this evening. As now, there had been portraits of ancestors hanging around the walls and there had been a silver candelabra on the table. For a brief moment the doctor was so confused that he no longer knew where he was. He was so ensnared in memory, that when they brought the injured man in and set him carefully down on the table, it did not seem real at all. Instinctively he sought for words to comfort the Countess, as he had done all those years ago, until all at once he realised it was not her son lying there, and that instead of the youthful Countess of long ago, it was an old woman with white ringlets who was standing by the table.

A revelation, faster than thought and too fast for him to grasp it properly, flashed through his mind, leaving in its wake a dull sense, rapidly fading, that 'time' is nothing more than a fiendish comedy, which an all-powerful, invisible enemy conjures up in the human brain.

One fruit of this insight remained: for a split second he had experienced from within something which until then he had not been capable of understanding properly, namely the strange, disconcerting moods of the Countess, who would sometimes see historical events from the time of her forebears as belonging to the present, and weave them inextricably into her everyday life.

It was as if he were responding to an irresistible urge when he shouted, "Water, bandages", and when – as all those years ago – he bent down and reached for the lancet which, out of long-redundant habit, he still carried in his breast pocket.

He only really regained his composure when he felt the breath from the mouth of the unconscious man on his exploring fingers and his eye chanced to fall on Božena's naked white thighs – with the lack of inhibition characteristic of Bohemian peasant girls, she had tucked up her skirts and squatted down to get a better view. At the shock of the contrast between blooming young life, the deathly rigor of the unconscious man, the ghostly figures of the ancestors on the walls and the wrinkled, senile features of the Countess, the image from the past concealing the present dissolved like a veil of mist before the sun.

The valet put the burning candelabra on the floor, from where its light illuminated the singular features of the unconscious man: his lips were ashen and formed an unnatural contrast with the bright-red make-up on his cheeks, making him look more like a wax figure from a fairground than a human being.

"Holy Saint Wenceslas, it's Zrcadlo!" exclaimed the maid, modestly pulling her skirt down below the knee, as if she felt the flickering light made the portrait of the page in its niche in the wall look as if he were casting a lustful eye on her.

"Who is it?" asked the Countess in surprise.

"Zrcadlo – the 'mirror' ", explained the valet, translating the Czech name. "That's what we all call him up here on the Hradschin, but I don't know if that's what he's really called. He's a lodger with ..." he paused in embarrassment, "with ... well, with Lizzie the Czech."

"With whom?"

The maid giggled behind her hand and the rest of the servants found it difficult to repress their laughter.

The Countess stamped her foot. "I want to know who with!"

The injured man was already giving the first signs of life, grinding his teeth, and it was Halberd who looked up and answered. "In her youth Lizzie the Czech was a celebrated ... er ... courtesan. I had no idea she was still alive and kicking on the Hradschin; she must be ancient. I presume she lives ..."

"... in Totengasse, where all the bad girls live", Božena hastened to explain.

"Well go and fetch the woman", ordered the Countess. Obediently the girl rushed out.

Meanwhile the man had recovered consciousness; he stared at the flickering candles for a while, then stood up slowly, without taking the least notice of his surroundings.

"Do you think he was trying to break in?" the Countess asked the servants in a low voice.

The valet shook his head and tapped his forehead, indicating he thought the man was mad.

"My opinion is that it is a case of sleep-walking", said the Penguin. "At full moon people who are susceptible tend to be seized by an inexplicable urge which makes them, without their being aware of it, do all kinds of strange things: climb up trees, houses and walls, and often they will walk along the narrowest of ledges at dizzying heights – on roof gutters, for example – with a surefootedness which they would certainly lack if they were awake." He turned to his patient, "Hey, you! Pane Zrcadlo, do you think you have gathered your wits enough to be able to find your way home?"

The somnambulist gave no reply, although he did seem to have heard the question, if not understood it, for he slowly turned his head towards the doctor and stared at him with empty, unmoving eyes.

Halberd drew back involuntarily, rubbed his forehead a few times, as if he were rummaging through his memories, then murmured, "Zrcadlo? No, I've never heard the name, but I have seen this man before. Where can it have been?"

The intruder was tall and gaunt, with a sallow complexion; his head was covered in a tangle of long, dry, grey locks. The violence of the contrast between his thin, clean-shaven face with the sharp Roman nose, sloping forehead, sunken temples and pinched lips and the make-up on his cheeks and his black cloak of threadbare velvet made him look like a figure out of a nightmare rather than a living human being.

'He looks like an old Egyptian Pharaoh who has disguised himself as an actor to hide the fact that it is a mummy under the make-up', was the bizarre thought that crept into the Penguin's mind. 'Incredible that I can't remember where I've seen that face before, it's striking enough.'

"The fellow's dead", grunted the Countess, half to herself, half to the Penguin, as she went up to the man standing in front of her and scrutinised his face from close to through her lorgnette with as little concern as if she were examining a statue. "Only a corpse could have such shrunken pupils. It doesn't seem to be able to move a single muscle, Halberd. Stop quivering like an old woman, Konstantin", she shouted at the dining-room door, which had slowly opened a crack to reveal the pale, terrified faces of Schirnding and Baron Elsenwanger. "Come in now, the pair of you, can't you see he doesn't bite."

The name of Konstantin seemed to have the effect of a psychological shock on the stranger. For a moment he trembled violently from head to toe, and his expression changed with lightning rapidity, like someone with incredible muscular control pulling faces in front of the mirror. As if his nose, jaw and cheekbones had suddenly become soft and pliable under the skin, his features slowly changed by gradual, bizarre stages, from the arrogant mask of an Egyptian king to a face that bore an unmistakable resemblance to the Elsenwanger family type.

It took scarcely a minute for this physiognomy to replace his former appearance and fix itself in his features so that, to their astonishment, the others seemed to see a completely different person before them. His head lolling on his chest and his left cheek swollen up as if by an abscess, so that the eye looked small and piercing, he trotted bow-legged up and down beside the table for a while, his lower lip stuck out, as if he were unsure what to do; then he felt all over his body for his pockets and rummaged in them.

Finally he saw Baron Elsenwanger, who was clutching onto Schirnding's arm, speechless with horror, nodded to him and said in a bleating voice, "Konstantindl, just the man, I've been looking for you all evening."

"Jesus, Mary and Joseph", howled the Baron, fleeing to the door, "death is in the house. Help, help, it's my dead brother, it's Bogumil!"

Von Schirnding, Dr. Halberd and the Countess all started at the sound of the somnambulist's voice: all three had known Baron Bogumil Elsenwanger when he was alive, and that was his voice exactly.

Without bothering about them in the least, Zrcadlo busied himself about the room, moving imaginary objects, picking them up and putting them down; only he could see them, but so vivid, so suggestive were his gestures that they took on visible form for his audience. When he suddenly listened, pursed his lips and trotted over to the window, whistling a few notes, took an imaginary mealworm out of an equally imaginary box and held it out to his pet starling, they were all so completely under his spell that for the moment they had forgotten where they were and been transported back to the time when the late Baron Bogumil Elsenwanger still lived there.

But when Zrcadlo, coming back from the window, stepped into the candlelight again and the sight of his shabby black velvet cloak destroyed the illusion for a second, they were seized with horror and waited, dumb and unresisting, to see what he would do next.

Zrcadlo thought for a while, repeatedly taking pinches of snuff from an invisible box, then put one of the carved chairs at an imaginary table in the middle of the room. Then he took an imaginary quill, cut it and split it – again with such frightening realism that they fancied they could even hear the squeak of the penknife – sat down and, with his head bent over on one side, began to write in the air. The Baron and his guests looked on with bated breath – at a wave from the Penguin the servants had tiptoed out of the room some time before – the only sounds breaking the deathly hush being the occasional groans from Elsenwanger, who could not tear his eyes away from his 'dead brother'.

Finally Zrcadlo seemed to have finished the letter, or whatever he was writing, for they could clearly see him make an elaborate flourish, presumably under his signature. He pushed his chair back noisily, went to the wall and searched for a long time in one of the niches with the pictures until he actually found what he must have been looking for, a key. Then he twisted one of the wooden rosettes, opened a lock that appeared behind it, pulled out a drawer, put his 'letter' in it and pushed the drawer back into the wall.

The tension among the onlookers had reached such a point that none of them heard Božena calling in a low voice from the next room, "Milostpane – Sir, may we come in now?"

"Did you see that? Halberd, did you see that too? Was that not a real drawer my late brother opened there?" It was Baron Elsenwanger who broke the silence, stuttering and sobbing with agitation. "I had no idea there was a drawer there." Wailing and wringing his hands he burst out, "Lord sakes, Bogumil, I never did anything to you! Saint Wenceslas preserve us, perhaps he's disinherited me because I haven't been to the Týn Church for thirty years!"

The doctor was about to go over to the wall and see if there really was a drawer, but he was interrupted by a loud knocking.

Immediately a tall, thin female dressed in rags appeared in the room and was announced by Božena as 'Lizzie the Czech'.

Her dress had once been an elegant gown, and its cut and the way it fell around her shoulders and hips still spoke of the care with which it had been made. The trimming at the neck and sleeves was genuine Brussels lace, though now it was stiff with

dirt and so crumpled as to be unrecognisable. The woman must
have been well into her seventies but, in spite of the awful
devastation caused by suffering and poverty, her features still
revealed traces of her former beauty. A certain self-confidence
in her manner and the calm, almost mocking eye she cast on the
three men – she did not deign to look at Countess Zahradka at
all – suggested she was in no way intimidated by the surroundings.

To judge by her meaningful grin, she seemed to be revelling
in the embarrassment of the three men, who obviously knew her
from her younger days rather more intimately than they would
like to admit before the Countess. But when Halberd began an
incomprehensible stuttering, she cut him short with a defer-
ential question, "You sent for me, gentlemen; may I know the
reason?"

Astounded by her unusually pure German and melodious, if
somewhat husky voice, the Countess raised her lorgnette and
scrutinised the prostitute with a glittering eye. Her female
instinct immediately told her what was the true reason for the
men's embarrassment and she saved the rather delicate situation
with a rapid succession of sharp counter-questions:

"This fellow here" – she pointed to Zrcadlo, who was standing motionless with his face to the wall in front of the portrait
of the blond-haired rococo lady – "has broken in. Who is he?
What does he want? I'm told he lives with you; what's the matter
with him? Is he mad? Or dr-" she could not bring herself to say
the word, and the mere memory of what they had just seen
brought back the horror, "or ... or ... I mean ... is he ... ill perhaps?
Has he the fever?"

Lizzie the Czech shrugged her shoulders and turned slowly
to face her questioner. Her eyes, beneath the inflamed lids bare
of lashes, seemed to be looking into empty space, as if there were
no one where the words had come from, and their expression
was so arrogant and contemptuous that the Countess felt the
blood rising to her cheeks.

"He fell off the garden wall", interjected the Penguin quickly.

27

"We thought at first he was dead, and so we sent for you. Who he is ... and what he is", he continued in desperation, trying to defuse the situation, "is neither here nor there. What he does appear to be, is a somnambulist, and you'll have to keep an eye on him at night so that he doesn't go off again. But now perhaps you would be good enough to take him back home. That is all right, isn't it, Baron?"

"Yes, yes, take him away", whimpered Elsenwanger. "Oh my God, just get rid of him!"

"All I know is that he is called Zrcadlo and is probably an actor", said Lizzie the Czech calmly. "At nights he goes round the inns and puts on performances for people. But", she shook her head, "no one has been able to find out whether he knows who he is himself. And I do not concern myself with who or what my tenants are. I don't pry. Come on, Pane Zrcadlo, it's time to go home. Can't you see that this isn't an inn?"

She went over to the somnambulist and took him by the hand.

Unresisting, he let himself be led to the door.

His similarity to the late Baron Bogumil had completely disappeared from his features; his figure seemed taller and more erect, his step sure, and his normal consciousness seemed to have more or less returned, even though he still took no notice of the others present, as if his senses were closed to the outside world, like those of a man who has been hypnotised.

The arrogant expression of an Egyptian king had also gone from his face. All that was left was an actor – but what an actor! A mask of flesh and blood that could be stretched into another, incomprehensible face every second; a mask such as Death himself would wear, if he should decide to mingle with the living. 'The face of a being,' felt Dr. Halberd, who was once more prey to a vague fear that he must have seen this person somewhere before, 'who can be *this* man today and someone completely different tomorrow, someone different not only for those around him, but also for himself; a corpse that does not decay and is a channel for invisible influences floating round in space; a creature that is not only called the 'mirror' but perhaps really is one.'

Lizzie the Czech had ushered the somnambulist out of the room and Halberd had taken the opportunity to whisper to her, "Off you go now, Lisinka; I'll come and see you tomorrow. But don't tell anyone. I must find out more about this Zrcadlo."

Then he stood for a while in the doorway, listening to see if they would talk to each other, but all he heard was the repeated encouragement of the woman, "There we go, there we go, Pane Zrcadlo. You can see this isn't an inn."

When he turned round, he saw that the rest had already gone into the neighbouring room and were sitting at the card-table, waiting for him. By their pale faces and agitated expressions he could tell that his friends' minds were not on the cards, and that it was only the imperious command of the strong-willed old lady that had made them return to their habitual evening diversion as if nothing had happened.

Chapter Two

The New World

The Penguin's ancestors had been personal physicians to the imperial family since time immemorial, and there was a saying current among the aristocratic circles on the castle hill in Prague that 'Halberds' had hung over all the crowned heads of Bohemia like swords of Damocles, ready to fall on their victims the moment they showed the least signs of illness. This special connection with the imperial house seemed confirmed by the fact that, after the death of the Dowager Empress Maria Anna, the Halberd family, the last scion of which was the confirmed bachelor, Dr. Thaddaeus Halberd known as the 'Penguin', was also doomed to extinction.

His nocturnal encounter with the sleepwalking Zrcadlo had brought an unwelcome disturbance into his bachelor existence which, until then, had been as regular as clockwork. His slumbers had been thronged with all sorts of dream-images, from which voluptuous memories of his youth gradually detached themselves, memories in which the charms of Lizzie the Czech – from the days, of course, when she was young and desirable – played a not inconsiderable role. A teasing tangle of fantasies, which reached its climax in the unaccustomed feeling that he was holding an alpenstock in his hand, woke him at an unwarrantably early hour.

Every year in the early summer – on June 1st, to be precise – it was Dr. Halberd's invariable custom to travel to Karlsbad to take the waters and, since he abhorred the railway, which he regarded as a Jewish affair, he used a cab for the journey. The first overnight stop was always made when Karlitschek, the grey nag which had the privilege of pulling the carriage, urged on by the insistent directions of the venerable, red-waistcoated coachman, reached Holleschowitz, a suburb five miles out of Prague. The next day the three-week journey was continued, in longer or shorter stages according to the mood of the noble steed. Once they had reached the spa, Karlitschek could feed itself up on oats until the journey home, by which time it was round and fat, like a pink, gleaming sausage on four thin stilts; during their stay, the former Physician to the Imperial Family prescribed pedestrian exercise for himself.

The appearance of May 1st in red on the tear-off calendar over his bed was the usual sign that it was high time to start packing his trunks and cases, but this morning the Penguin ignored it completely, left April 30th, with the eerie legend 'Walpurgisnacht', undisturbed, and went over to his desk, where he took out a gigantic tome bound in pigskin with brass corners, which had been used as a diary by all male Halberds from the time of his great-grandfather. He started looking through the entries, to see if they might contain any clues as to when and where he might have met the mysterious Zrcadlo before, for he was tormented by the idea that that must be the case.

Every morning since his twenty-fifth year, starting on the day his father had died, he had punctiliously entered the events of the previous day, just as his ancestors had done and continuing the serial numbers they had used: the current day was No. 16,117.

As he could not have known that he would remain a bachelor and therefore leave no family after his death, he had – again following the example of his ancestors – from the very beginning used a secret code and signs, which only he could decipher, for anything connected with his amorous exploits.

To his credit, it must be admitted that the number of such passages in the book was relatively low; the ratio of their frequency, compared to the goulashes consumed at Schnell's, which he was equally conscientious in recording, was of the order of 1:300.

In spite of the scrupulous care with which the diary had been kept, Halberd could find no passage that had the remotest connection with the somnambulist and, with a sigh of disappointment, he closed the book.

Leafing through its pages, he had felt a disagreeable sensation creep over him; as he read through the individual entries he had gradually become aware – for the very first time – of how inexpressibly monotonous his life had been. At other times it had been his pride that he boasted a way of life that was more regular and self-enclosed than that of almost any of the exclusive aristocratic circles in the Hradschin, and that his blood, although not blue, had, over the generations, rid itself of all impetuosity, of all plebeian desire for progress. Now, however, while he was still under the impression of the events of the previous night in Elsenwanger House, he suddenly felt that a desire had awoken within him which could only be described by unpleasant words, words such as: dissatisfaction, curiosity, the lust for adventure, the urge to investigate inexplicable events.

Puzzled, he looked round the room. The undecorated, white-washed walls irritated him. They had never done that before. Why suddenly now?

He was annoyed with himself.

His three rooms were in the southern wing of the royal castle; they had been allocated to him on his retirement by the Imperial and Royal Chamberlain's Office. From a balcony, on which stood a powerful telescope, he could see down into the 'world' – Prague – and beyond, on the horizon, he could just make out the woods and gentle undulations of the green hills, whilst another window gave a view up the Moldau, a glittering, silvery ribbon that disappeared in the hazy distance.

To calm down his errant thoughts a little, he went over to the telescope and focused it on the city, allowing, as usual, chance to dictate the precise part he would see. The instrument had a remarkable degree of magnification and, therefore, only a tiny field of vision, consequently the objects were brought so close to the eye of the observer that they seemed to be immediately in front of him.

Halberd bent down to the eyepiece with an instinctive secret wish, which he scarcely allowed himself to acknowledge, namely that he would see a chimney-sweep on a roof, or some other traditional omen of good luck. Instead, he immediately drew back with an expression of horror: Lizzie the Czech had appeared, as large as life, her face twisted in a spiteful grin and winking with her bare lids, as if she had seen and recognised him!

It was such a tremendous shock, that Halberd was trembling all over, and for a while he stared in consternation past the telescope out into the heat haze, expecting every second to see the old hag appear in person, perhaps even as a ghost riding on a broomstick.

When he finally pulled himself together, still surprised at the bizarre trick chance had played on him, but happy to allow a natural explanation, he looked through the telescope again: the old woman had disappeared and only unknown faces of no interest to him passed across his field of vision; but he still felt that there was a strange excitement in their faces, a tension, which communicated itself to him.

By the haste with which they elbowed each other out of the way, by their gestures, their chattering lips and the way they sometimes opened their mouths wide, as if they were shouting something, he realised that he must be witnessing some kind of assembly, although because of the distance he could not determine what had caused it. A little tug on the telescope and the picture disappeared, to be replaced by another, rather blurred at first, a dark rectangular something which gradually, as he adjusted the lens, turned into an open gable window with newspaper stuck over the broken panes.

A young woman clothed in rags, her haggard features sunk to an almost corpse-like gauntness, her eyes deep in their sockets, was framed by the window, sitting with her dull gaze fixed in brutish apathy on a little, skeleton-thin child, that had obviously just died in her arms. The glaring sunlight that fell on the pair showed up every detail with cruel clarity and, with its jubilant spring radiance, heightened the contrast between joy and misery so much that it was unbearable.

"The war. Yes indeed, the war", sighed the Penguin, and gave the tube a push so that the terrible sight would not unnecessarily spoil his appetite for lunch.

"That must be the rear entrance to a theatre, or something of the kind", he murmured pensively as a new scene appeared before him: watched by countless street urchins and bobbing old ladies in headscarves, two workmen were carrying an enormous painting out of a yawning gateway; it depicted an old man with a long white beard, lying on pink clouds, an expression of indescribable tenderness in his eyes, his right hand outstretched in blessing, whilst the left was tenderly clasping a globe.

Not very satisfied, and tormented by conflicting emotions, Dr. Halberd returned to his room, received his housekeeper's announcement that 'Wenceslas was waiting outside' without a word, took his top hat, gloves and ivory cane and made his way with creaking joints down the chilly stone stairs and out into the castle courtyard, where the coachman was already busy taking down the roof of his cab, in order to allow his employer to stow his long limbs in the interior of the carriage without bumping himself.

The cab had rattled most of the way down the steep street when a thought suddenly occurred to the Penguin which caused him to tap at the rickety windows until Karlitschek finally condescended to make his front legs go rigid, thus bringing the coach to an abrupt halt. Wenceslas jumped down from the box and, hat in hand, opened the door.

As if they had sprung up from the ground, a horde of schoolboys immediately thronged round the cab and, when they saw who was inside, performed in his honour a kind of silent penguin dance, clumsily flapping their bent arms and pecking at each other with imaginary long, pointed beaks. Halberd ignored the mocking children and whispered something to the cabbie which for a moment made him literally freeze.

"What, your Excellency? Your Excellency wants me to drive you to Totengasse?" he finally managed to bring out. "To the ... to the ... to the whores? This early in the day?"

"But Lizzie the Czech don't live there", he explained in relief, when the Penguin had told him more precisely what he intended. "Lizzie the Czech lives in the New World, thank the Lord."

"In the ... 'world'? Down there?" rejoined Halberd, casting a sour glance out of the window at the city spread out at his feet.

"In the *New World*", said the cabbie in soothing tones, "In that alley what goes round outside of the Stag Moat." To emphasise his explanation he jerked his thumb up towards the sky, describing a circle in the air with his arm, as if the old woman lived in an almost inaccessible abode, in the astral realm, so to speak, between heaven and earth.

A few minutes later the faithful Karlitschek, with the slow, measured tread of a Caucasian mountain mule, was making its way back up the steep Spornergasse. What had occurred to Halberd was that he had seen Lizzie the Czech through his telescope in the streets of Prague barely half an hour ago and that therefore it ought to be a favourable opportunity for a tête-à-tête with Zrcadlo, who lodged with her. He had therefore decided to seize the opportunity, even if it did mean missing his lunch at Schnell's.

When he reached the street called the New World – to avoid attracting embarrassing attention he had to leave the cab behind – the Penguin discovered that it consisted of a row of seven detached houses with a semicircular wall opposite, the top of which had been decorated with a frieze of illustrations, scribbled in chalk by a schoolboy hand, but nonetheless extremely explicit, depicting a variety of sexual activities. Apart from a few children, who were whipping tops in the ankle-deep dust of the alley, there was not a person to be seen.

A breeze redolent of jasmine and lilac wafted up from the Stag Moat, the sides of which were covered with flowering trees and shrubs, and in the distance, surrounded by the silvery-white spray from the fountains, the summer residence of Empress Anna with its swelling, green copper roof sat like a gigantic, gleaming beetle dreaming in the midday sunshine.

Halberd suddenly felt his heart beat louder in his breast. The soft, drowsy spring air, the intoxicating scent of the flowers, the children at play, the hazy glow of the city at his feet, and the towering cathedral with flocks of jackdaws squawking in their nests: it all reawakened in him the dull feeling of self-reproach he had had that morning, as if he had cheated his soul of its life.

For a while he watched the clouds of dust whirled up by the little red and grey tops as they spun under the whips. He could not remember ever having played with them himself as a child, and now he felt that through that omission he had missed a life full of happiness.

There were no signs of life in the open hallways of the little houses into which he peeped to find out where Zrcadlo lived. In one of them stood an empty, glass-fronted wooden stand from which, in peacetime, they probably sold rolls covered in blue-black poppy seeds or, as a dried-out wooden barrel suggested, the liquid that pickled gherkins had been kept in; it was a local speciality: for a copper you could pull the leather belt that was left hanging in the juice twice through your mouth.

Outside another house entrance was a badly scratched black and yellow sign with a double-headed eagle on it and the remains of an inscription announcing that the occupants were licensed purveyors of salt to the public.

It all exuded a feeling of melancholy, as if it belonged to the past. Even the notice with large, once-black letters saying 'Zde se mandluje', which was as much as to say that for a modest fee, paid in advance, servant-girls could use the mangle for an hour, clearly indicated that the owner of that enterprise must have lost all confidence in his source of income.

Everywhere the pitiless hand of the war-god had passed, leaving destruction in its wake.

The Penguin decided to try his luck with the last of the row of shacks, from which a thin snake of grey-blue smoke was curling up into the cloudless May sky. When his repeated knocking remained unanswered, he opened the door and, an unpleasant surprise, found himself face to face with Lizzie the Czech, who, a wooden bowl full of bread soup on her knees, recognised him immediately and welcomed him with a delighted cry of, "Well hello! Penguin! Is that really you?!"

The room, which served at one and the same time as kitchen, living-room and, to judge by a pile of old rags, bundles of straw and screwed-up newspaper in the corner, bedroom, was indescribably filthy and neglected. Everything – table, chairs, chest of drawers, crockery – was in disorder; amid the dismal clutter the only bright spot was Lizzie the Czech herself, who was clearly overjoyed at her unexpected visitor.

Along the walls, with their tattered Pompeian red wallpaper, hung a row of withered laurel wreaths with faded, pale blue silk sashes, on which were written such things as 'To a Great Artiste'; below them was a beribboned mandoline.

With the natural self-assurance of a great lady, Lizzie the Czech remained calmly seated and, with a winning smile, held out her hand, which Halberd, flushing blood-red with embarrassment, took and squeezed, but could not bring himself to kiss.

Graciously ignoring this lack of gallantry, Lizzie the Czech opened the conversation with a few remarks on the fine weather they had been having, at the same time finishing her soup and assuring the doctor how much pleasure it gave her to receive a visit from such a dear old friend.

"You always were a damned fine figure of a man, Penguin", she said, suddenly slipping from the urbane to the intimate, and then into the local patois, "a *sakramentsky chlap*."

She seemed overcome by memory and was silent for a moment, her eyes closed, as if to hold in the wistful recollections. Halberd waited, on tenterhooks for what she was going to say next.

Suddenly she puckered her lips and purred huskily, "Embrasse-moi, embrasse-moi", spreading her arms wide.

With a shudder of revulsion, Halberd shrank back and stared at her in horror, but she ignored him, rushed over to the sideboard, picked up a picture – a faded daguerreotype – from the many that were propped up there, and covered it with passionate kisses. He gasped when he recognised the portrait of himself he had given her a good forty years ago. Then carefully, tenderly, she replaced it, coyly took the hem of her skirts between finger and thumb, raised it to her knees and danced a ghostly gavotte, rocking her head, with its tangle of unkempt hair, back and forward, as if lost in voluptuous dreams.

The Penguin was rooted to the spot, the room seemed to be turning; *danse macabre* was the phrase that came to his mind, and he seemed to see the two words in fancy lettering under an old copper engraving that he had once found in an antique shop.

He could not tear his eyes away from the old woman's skinny, skeletal legs in their wrinkled stockings that had once been black but now had a shiny, greenish tinge. So great was the abhorrence he felt, that he wanted to flee through the door, but he found he could not: he was spellbound by a fusion of past and present in a vision of ghastly reality which he felt powerless to escape. Was he still young, and had the beautiful girl dancing before him been transformed in a flash into a corpselike old hag with toothless jaws and wrinkled, inflamed eyelids? Or was he dreaming, and had neither of them ever been young?

Those shapeless lumps in the dingy grey, mouldy remains of worn-out shoes, twirling and skipping before his eyes – could they really be the same delicate little feet with the trim ankles which had once so delighted and enthralled him?

'She can't have taken them off for years, the leather would have fallen to pieces. She must sleep in them', was the thought that whispered through his mind, to be driven away by another, 'How terrible that we should decay in the invisible tomb of time, even while we are still alive.'

"Do you remember, Thaddaeus?" warbled Lizzie in her hoarse voice, and started to croak out a song:

> "Cold as the snow,
> You set me on fire;
> Your kiss makes the ice
> Burn with desire."

Then all at once, as if she suddenly remembered who and where she was, she stopped, flung herself into the armchair and, overwhelmed by a sudden flood of anguish, curled up, hiding the tears pouring down her face behind her hands.

Halberd awoke from the spell, roused himself and for a moment regained control over himself, only to lose it again immediately: he had suddenly remembered his uneasy slumbers the previous night; with vivid clarity he relived the dream of a few hours ago in which he had embraced this wrinkled body, covered in rags and heaving with uncontrollable sobs, as a young woman in the flower of her beauty.

He opened and closed his mouth a few times, but no words came out, he had no idea what to say.

"Lizzie", he finally managed to stutter, "Lizzie, are things really so bad?" His eye travelled round the room and fixed on the wooden soup-bowl. "Lizzie, is there any way I can help you?" 'She used to eat from silver plates and ...' with a shudder he shot a glance at the filthy bedclothes, 'and sleep in a feather-bed.'

Without looking up, the old woman shook her head violently.

Halberd could hear her trying to control her whimpering behind her hands.

His photograph on the sideboard was looking him straight in the eye, the reflection from a clouded mirror by the window sent a beam of light slanting across the whole row: slim, young men-about-town, all of whom he had known, and some of whom he still knew as stiff and white-haired princes and barons; he himself had a merry laugh in his eyes, gold braid on his coat and a three-cornered hat under his arm.

When he had first seen his photograph here he had had the idea of removing it secretly, should the opportunity arise; automatically, he took a step towards it, but immediately stopped, ashamed of himself.

The old woman's back and shoulders were still heaving with repressed sobs; he looked down at her, and felt a warm wave of pity flood through him. He forgot his disgust at her filthy hair and laid his hand on her head, hesitantly, as if he were unsure of himself; he even stroked it shyly. It seemed to calm her, and she gradually quietened down like a little child.

"Lizzie", he started again after a while, speaking very quietly, "Lizzie, look, you needn't worry about it ... if you ... I mean, if things are that bad ... You know ...", he was searching for the right words, "well, you know ... there's a war on, isn't there, and we all have to go hungry now and ... now that there's a war on ..." He gulped in his embarrassment, for he knew he was lying; he had never gone hungry, had no idea what it was like; every day at Schnell's they even secretly slipped freshly baked bread-sticks of white flour under his napkin. "Yes, well ... well now that I know how bad things are, you needn't worry any more, Lizzie; of course I'll help you, it says without going ... er ... saying ... And the war", he tried to cheer her up by sounding cheerful himself, "well, it might be over tomorrow, and then you can start earning ..." – he broke off in consternation; he suddenly remembered what she was and that there was hardly any question of 'earnings' from that source – "er ... hmm ... your living", he finished in a sheepish voice after a pause, as he couldn't think of a better word.

She grabbed his hand and kissed it silently and gratefully. He could feel the tear-drops falling on his fingers. "Oh, come now", he wanted to say, but could not bring out the words. He looked around, at a complete loss.

For a while both were silent. The he heard her mumbling something, but could not understand the words.

"Thththank yyyou", she finally sobbed, her voice half stifled by tears, "ththank you, Pen ... thank you, Thaddaeus. No, no money", she went on hastily, when he started to go on again about helping her, "no, there's nothing I need." She sat up quickly, turning her head to the wall so that he should not see her anguished face, but still kept a tight hold of his hand. "Things are not that bad. I'm so happy that you could bear to touch me. No, no, really, I'm quite well off, only ... you know it's so terrible when you remember how everything used to be." For a

40

moment she gulped again and clasped her throat, as if she had difficulty breathing. "You know, the terrible thing is that ... that you never grow old."

The Penguin gave her a startled look and thought at first that she was starting to ramble, but as she went on, more calmly now, he gradually came to understand what she meant:

"Before, when you came in, I thought I was young again, Thaddaeus ... and you were still in love with me", she added softly. "It often happens, sometimes ... sometimes even for a whole quarter of an hour. Especially when I'm out in the streets, I forget who I am and think that people are looking at me because I'm young and beautiful. Then, of course, when I hear what the children shout after me ..." She buried her face in her hands again.

"Don't take it to heart so, Lizzie", Halberd tried to comfort her, "children are always cruel, they don't realise what they are doing. You shouldn't hold it against them, and if they see that you don't care ..."

"Do you think I get angry with them? I've never been angry with anyone. Not even with God, and nowadays everyone has good reason to be angry with Him. No, that's not it. It's the waking up, Thaddaeus, every time, from a beautiful dream, it's worse than being burnt alive."

The Penguin looked round the room again with an appraising glance. 'If we could make things a bit more comfortable for her here', he thought, 'perhaps she would ...'

She seemed to have guessed his thoughts. "You wonder why it's so awful here and why I don't look after myself any more? God, how often have I tried to tidy the room up a bit. But whenever I do, I feel I'm about to go mad. I only have to begin to straighten up a chair, and something inside me starts screaming that things can never be what they were. There are probably a lot of people who are just as badly off, but they can never understand those of us who have sunk from the heights to the very depths. You won't believe this, Thaddaeus, but it's true; it's a kind of comfort to me that everything around, myself included, is so squalid and disgusting." For a while she stared into space, then she suddenly burst out, "And I know the reason. Why should people not be forced to live in squalor, when their souls are stuck in these horrible corpses! ... And then, in the middle of all this filth here", she muttered to herself, "perhaps I'll manage to forget sometime." She started talking to herself, as if her thoughts were wandering. "If it wasn't for that Zrcadlo!" The Penguin pricked up his ears when he heard the name, and it came back to him that it was actually to see the actor that he had come here. "Yes, if it wasn't for Zrcadlo! I'm sure it's all his fault. I'll have to send him away. If only ... if only I had the strength to do it."

Halberd coughed to attract her attention. "Tell me, Lizzie, who is this Zrcadlo?" Finally he asked her straight out, "He lodges with you, doesn't he?"

She rubbed her forehead. "Zrcadlo? What makes you ask about him?"

"Nothing. Just curious. After what happened yesterday at Elsenwanger's. I'm interested in him. As a doctor, you know."

Lizzie slowly focused on her surroundings again, then her eyes suddenly filled with terror. She grasped Halberd by the sleeve. "Do you know, sometimes I think he's the Devil. Holy Mother of God, Thaddaeus, keep him out of your mind ... No, no", she gave a hysterical laugh, "that's all foolish talk. There's no such thing as the Devil ... He's mad, that's all there is to it ... or an actor ... or both at once." She tried to laugh again, but her lips stuck in a silent rictus.

Halberd saw that an icy shudder ran over her and her toothless jaws quivered.

"Of course he's ill", he said reassuringly. "But sometimes he must be in his right mind, and I'd just like to have a chat with him when he is."

"He's never in his right mind", muttered Lizzie.

"But last night you said he goes round the inns and puts on performances for people?"

"Yes, he does that."

"Well then, he must be in his right mind to do that?"

"No, he's not."

"Is that so? Hmm." The Penguin thought hard. "But he had make-up on yesterday. Does he do that without knowing what he's doing? Who puts it on for him?"

"I do."

"You do? What on earth for?"

"So people'll think he's an actor. So he can earn some money. And so they won't lock him away."

The Penguin gave her a long, hard look. 'He can't be her ... her pimp', he thought. His pity had vanished and he was filled with disgust again. 'She probably depends on his takings as well. Yes, of course, that'll be it.'

Lizzie the Czech had suddenly changed again, too. She had taken a piece of bread out of her pocket and was chewing at it grumpily.

In his embarrassment Halberd kept shifting his weight from one foot to another. He was beginning to be extremely annoyed with himself for having come here at all.

"If you want to go, it's not me what's keeping you", muttered the old woman, after both had been silent for an increasingly awkward time.

Relieved, Halberd quickly grabbed his hat and said, "You're quite right, of course, Lizzie, it is getting on. Yes ... er ... well, I'll pop round and see you again some time, Lizzie." He automatically felt for his purse.

"I've told you already, I don't want no money", hissed the old woman.

Halberd's hand jerked away from his pocket, and he turned to go, "Well then, all the best, Lizzie."

"Cheerio, Thadd –, cheerio Penguin."

The next moment he was out in the street, blinking in the bright sunlight and making his tetchy way to his cab, to escape from the New World and back to his lunch as quickly as possible.

Chapter Three

The Dalibor Tower

The shadows of the old lime trees were already slanting across the quiet, walled courtyard of the Dalibor Tower, the grey dungeon on the Hradschin. For a good hour now the tiny warden's cottage where the veteran soldier, Vondrejc, lived with his arthritic wife and his adopted son Ottokar, a nineteen-year old student at the conservatoire, had been enveloped in the cool afternoon shade.

The old man was sitting on a bench, counting copper and nickel coins, the tips that the day's visitors had given him, and sorting them into piles on the rotting wood beside him. Every time he reached ten, he made a line in the sand with his wooden leg.

He finished with a discontented grunt and muttered, "Two crowns, seventy-eight kreutzer", to his adopted son, who was leaning against a tree, desperately trying to brush out the shiny patches on the knees of his black suit; then he shouted it out loud, like a military report, through the open window, so that his bedridden wife could hear it in the living room.

That accomplished, Vondrejc, wearing his field-grey sergeant's cap on his completely bald head, sank into a deathlike stupor, like a jumping jack whose string had broken, his half-blind eyes fixed on the fallen blossoms strewn over the ground like so many dead damselflies.

He did not even move a muscle when his son picked up his violin-case from the bench, put on his velvet cap and made his way to the barrack-sized gate with its official yellow and black stripes. He did not even respond to his "Goodbye".

The violin student set off down the hill, towards Thungasse where Countess Zahradka lived in a narrow, dark town house. After a few seconds, however, he stopped, as if an idea had suddenly struck him, had a quick look at his scratched pocket-

44

watch, then hurried back up the hill, cutting the corners of the path up out of the Stag Moat as much as possible, to the New World, where, without knocking, he went into the room of Lizzie the Czech.

The old woman was so wrapped up in the memories of her youth, that it was a long time before she understood what he wanted.

"The future? What do you mean: the future?" she mumbled absent-mindedly, only taking in the last word of what he said. "The future? There's no such thing as the future!" Slowly she looked him up and down, obviously confused by his braided student's jacket. "Why don't they have gold braid nowadays? He is the Lord Chamberlain, you know", she said to the room at large in a low voice. "Oh! It's Pan Vondrejc mladší, young Mr. Vondrejc wants to know the future. So that's it." Only now did she realise whom she was talking to.

Without another word, she went over to the sideboard and fished out from under it a plank covered with reddish modelling clay, placed it on the table and handed Ottokar a wooden stylus, saying, "Now, Pane Vondrejc, prick it from right to left – but without counting! Just think of what you want to know. Do sixteen rows, one below the other."

Ottokar took the stylus, knitted his brows and hesitated for a while, then suddenly went deathly pale with excitement and, his hand trembling, feverishly stabbed the soft clay full of tiny holes.

He watched her eagerly as she counted them up, wrote them down in columns on a board and then drew geometrical shapes in a quadrilateral divided up into a number of squares, chattering mechanically all the while as she did so.

"These are the mothers, the daughters, the nephews, the witnesses, the Red Man, the White Man and the Judge, the dragon's tail and the dragon's head, all just as they should be according to the good old Bohemian Art of the Dots. That what we learned from the Saracens, before they were wiped out in the Battle on the White Mountain. Long before Queen Libussa. Yes, yes, the

White Mountain is soaked in human blood. Bohemia is the source of all wars. It was this time and it always will be. Our leader Jan Žižka, Žižka the Blind."

"What's that about Žižka?" Ottokar interrupted feverishly, "Does it say anything about Žižka?"

She ignored his question. "If the Moldau did not flow so fast it would still be red with blood, even today." Then all at once she changed her tone, speaking as if in bitter amusement, "Do you know, my son, why there are so many leeches in the Moldau? From the source until it flows into the Elbe, wherever you lift up a stone on the bank, you will always find little leeches underneath. That's because at one time it was a river of blood. And they are waiting because they know that the day will come when it will feed them again ... What is that?" With a cry of astonishment she dropped the chalk and looked from the figures on the board to the young man and back again. "What's that? You want to become Emperor of the World?" She looked searchingly into his dark, flickering eyes.

He gave no answer, but she noticed that he was clutching the table to stop himself falling. "Would it be because of that woman there?" she said, pointing to one of the geometrical figures. "And I always thought you were sweet on that Božena from Baron Elsenwanger's?"

Ottokar gave a violent shake of the head.

"Is that so? It's all over is it, son? Don't worry, a real Czech girl never bears a grudge, even if she's pregnant. But you beware of *her*", again she pointed to the shape, "she's a bloodsucker. She's Czech as well, but she belongs to the old race, the dangerous race."

"That's not true", said Ottokar in a hoarse voice.

"She is of the blood of the Bořivoj, I tell you. And you", she gave the young man's narrow, brown face a long, thoughtful look, "you are of the Bořivoj line as well. Two such as you are drawn together like iron and magnet. There's no need to waste my time reading the signs", and she wiped her arm over the board before Ottokar could stop her. "Just you be careful it's not

46

you that's the iron and she the magnet, otherwise you're lost, son. Murder and incest were standard practice among the Bořivoj. Remember Good King Wenceslas!"

Ottokar tried to smile. "Saint Wenceslas was no more from the line of Bořivoj than I am. My name is Vondrejc, Frau ... Frau Lisinka."

"Don't keep on calling me Frau Lisinka!" In her fury the old woman thumped the table with her fist. "I'm no Frau, I'm a whore!"

"What I would like to know ... er, Lisinka, is what you meant by 'becoming Emperor of the World' and what you said about Jan Žižka?" asked Ottokar timidly.

A creaking noise from behind made him stop. He turned round to see the door slowly open and in the frame a man appeared with a large pair of dark spectacles on his face, an incredibly long coat, which had something carelessly stuffed between the shoulders to make him look like a hunchback, his nostrils flared wide from cotton wool that had been stuffed up them, and a carroty wig and whiskers which one could tell from a hundred yards were stuck on.

"Prosím. Milostpane. Milady." The stranger addressed Lizzie the Czech in a voice that was obviously disguised. "Do hexcuse me, Ma'am, for the disturbance, but would I be right in thinkin' that 'is Majesty's Physician, Doctor von 'Alberd was 'ere a while ago?"

The old woman twisted her mouth in a silent grin.

"Do hexcuse the hinterruption, but I did 'ear 'e was 'ere, Ma'am."

Still nothing but the corpse-like grin. The strange visitor was clearly perplexed.

"You see, I 'ave to hinform 'is Excellency –"

"I don't know of any Majesty's Physician", Lizzie the Czech suddenly yelled at him. "Get out, and make it quick, you pest."

Like lightning, the door was shut, and the dripping sponge that the old woman had taken from the slate and hurled at her visitor fell to the floor with a damp thud.

"That was only Stefan Brabetz", she said, anticipating Ottokar's question. "He's an informer, works on his own account. He dresses up differently every time and thinks nobody knows who he is. If there's anything going on, he soon picks it up. Then he'd like to demand money, but he doesn't know how to go about it. He comes from down below. From Prague. They're all like that down there. I think it must be a result of the mysterious air that comes up out of the ground. They all become like him in time, some sooner, some later – unless they die first. Whenever they meet someone, they give a sly grin, so the other will believe they know something about them. Have you never noticed, son" – she became oddly uneasy and began to walk restlessly up and down the room – "that everything is crazy in Prague? Crazy from all the secrecy? You're mad yourself, son, you just don't know it. Of course, up here on the Hradschin it's a different kind of madness. Quite different from down there. More a kind of ... of fossilised madness. Everything up here's turned into a fossil. But once the storm breaks, these giant fossils will come back to life and smash the city to smithereens ... At least", her voice sank to a low murmur, "that's what my grandmother used to tell me when I was a girl. Well, I suppose that Stefan Brabetz can smell that there's something in the air up here on the Hradschin. Something's going on."

Ottokar went pale and gave a shy, involuntary glance at the door. "How do you mean? What's supposed to be going on?"

Lizzie the Czech stared straight in front of her. "Yes, believe me, sonny, you're mad already. Perhaps you really do want to become Emperor of the World." She paused. "And why should it not be possible? If there weren't so many madmen in Prague, how could all the wars start there?! Yes, you stay mad, son. In the end why shouldn't a madman rule the world? Why, I became the mistress of King Milan Obrenović, simply by believing it was possible. And how close I was to being Queen of Serbia!" It was as if she suddenly woke up. "Why are you not in the war, son. Oh? A weak heart, is it? Hmm. And why do you think you are not a Bořivoj?" She gave him no time to answer. "And where are you off to now, sonny, with your violin?"

"To Countess Zahradka's. I'm to play to her."

The old woman gave him a surprised look and once more subjected his face to a long and detailed scrutiny, then, like someone who is now certain, she said, "Hmm. Well. Bořivoj. And does she like you, Countess Zahradka?"

"She's my godmother."

Lizzie the Czech laughed out loud. "Godmother, hahaha, godmother!"

Ottokar did not know what to make of her laughter. He would have liked to ask his question about Jan Žižka again, but he saw there was no point.

He had known the old woman too long not to be aware that her impatient expression meant that she wanted the interview to end. With a shy mumble of thanks, he slipped out of the door.

He had scarcely caught sight of the old Capuchin monastery dreaming in the glow of the setting sun, than he heard, just beside him as if in greeting, the ancient bells of the Loretto Church casting their spell over him like a magical orchestra of aeolian harps. The air, vibrant with melody and fragrant with the scent of the flowers in the nearby gardens, enfolded him in the gossamer caress of some invisible, ethereal realm. Enchanted, he stopped and listened, and seemed to hear the tones of an old hymn, sung by a thousand voices. And as he listened, he felt at times that it came from within him, then as if the notes were hovering round his head, to echo and die away in the clouds; sometimes it was so near, he thought he could recognise the Latin words of the psalm, at others, drowned by the sonorous boom of the bronze bells, it sounded like faint chords rising from underground cloisters.

Deep in thought, he crossed the Hradschin Square with its feast-day decoration of silver-birch twigs, passing in front of the Castle; the noise of the bells crashed in resounding waves against its rock-hewn ramparts, making his violin in its wooden case vibrate, like a body in a coffin coming back to life.

49

Then he was standing at the top of the New Castle Steps, looking down the balustrade-girt flight of two hundred granite steps onto a sea of sunlit roofs, from the depths of which, like a gigantic black caterpillar, a procession was crawling slowly up. It seemed to raise a silver head with purple-spotted feelers, searching for its way, as, under the white canopy carried by four priests in albs and stoles, the Prince-Archbishop, with the little red cap on his head, red silk shoes on his feet and gold-embroidered chasuble round his shoulders, led the singing crowd upwards, step by step.

In the warm, still evening air, the flames over the candles carried by the servers were almost invisible ovals trailing thin black threads of smoke through the bluish clouds from the swinging thuribles. The setting sun lay on the city, streaming over the long bridges in a blaze of crimson and flowing past the piers with the current, gold transformed into blood. It flared up in a thousand windows, as if the houses were on fire.

Ottokar stared at the scene; he could still hear the old woman's words, how she had said the Moldau once ran red with blood. And the magnificent spectacle of the procession coming ever closer up the Castle Steps! For a moment he was in a daze: that was how it would be, when his mad dream of being crowned emperor was fulfilled! He closed his eyes so as not to see the people who were standing beside him to watch the procession; for a few minutes more he wanted to block out the sight of the everyday world.

Then he turned round and passed through the Castle courtyards, in order to make his way to Thungasse by another, deserted route. As he came round the corner by the Provincial Diet he was surprised to see the huge gates of the Wallenstein Palace wide open. He hurried along, to try and catch a glimpse of the gloomy garden covered in ivy with branches as thick as a man's arm, and perhaps see the wonderful renaissance hall and the historic grotto behind it. As a child he had seen all these marvels from close to, and the memory was deeply engraved on his soul, as of a visit to a fairy kingdom.

Lackeys in silver-braided livery and with close-cropped whiskers and clean-shaven upper lips were silently dragging the stuffed horse, that had carried Wallenstein when it was alive, out into the street. He recognised it by the scarlet blanket and its staring yellow eyes, which, he suddenly remembered, had often appeared in his childhood sleep, as a mysterious omen which he had never been able to interpret.

Now the stallion stood before him in the golden-red rays of the setting sun, its hooves screwed to a dark-green board, like a gigantic toy sent from a dream-world to these prosaic times, to this age which has stolidly accepted the most terrible of all wars: the war of men against demonic machines, compared with which Wallenstein's battles seem no more than alehouse brawls.

Once again, as at the sight of the procession, an icy shiver ran down his spine when he saw the riderless horse that seemed only to be waiting for some determined man, some new master, to leap into the saddle. He did not hear the passers-by commenting disparagingly on its moth-eaten hide. The mocking question from one of the lackeys – "Would it perhaps please my Lord Marshal to mount?" – made his bowels churn and his hair stand on end, as if it were the voice of destiny coming from the primal depths. He was impervious to the scorn behind the servant's words. Only an hour ago, the old woman had said to him, "You're mad yourself, son, only you don't know it", but had she not gone on to say, "In the end, why shouldn't a madman rule the world"?

He could feel his heart beating in his throat with wild excitement; he tore himself away from his fantasies and raced to Thungasse.

When spring arrived, old Countess Zahradka used to move into the small, dark mansion of her late sister, Countess Morzin, where the rooms were never brightened by a single ray of light. She hated the sun and even more she hated the month of May, with its soft, voluptuous breath and the cheerful people in their

Sunday best. At that time, her own house, close to the Premonstratensian monastery at the highest point of the city, was fast asleep behind closed shutters. The stairs Ottokar was rushing up were of bare brick, and led, directly and without passing through a hall, into the stone-cold corridor with marble flags onto which the doors of the various rooms opened.

There were rumours – though God only knows where they came from – that the house, which resembled nothing more than a county courthouse, was haunted and, moreover, concealed an immense treasure. They had probably been invented by some wag to emphasise the contempt for all romantic fancies which seemed to emanate from its every stone. Ottokar's daydreams certainly vanished from his mind the moment he set foot on the steps. He was filled with such a sense of his own poverty-stricken insignificance that he gave an involuntary bow before he knocked and entered.

The room in which Countess Zahradka, sitting in a chair covered entirely in grey hessian, was waiting for him, was the most uncomfortable imaginable: the stove of Meissen porcelain, the sofas, sideboards, chairs, the chandelier of Venetian glass, that must have had a hundred candles, a suit of armour, were all covered with sheets, as if awaiting an auction; even the countless miniatures, which covered the walls from ceiling to floor, were veiled in gauze; 'to keep the flies off', Ottokar remembered the Countess telling him when once, as a child, he had asked her about the reason for these bizarre protective covers. Or had he only dreamed it? The many times he had been here he could never remember having seen a single fly.

He had often wondered what might be outside the clouded window-panes, by which the old lady used to sit. Could it be a courtyard, a garden, a street? He had never attempted to ascertain what it was; to do so, he would have had to go past the Countess, and the very idea was unthinkable. The eternal sameness of the room stifled any resolutions he might have made. The moment he entered, he was transported back to the time when he had had to make his first visit here, and he felt as if he himself were sewn up in hessian and linen, to protect him against non-existent flies.

The only object that was not draped, or at least only partially so, was the one life-sized portrait among all the miniatures; a rectangular hole had been cut in the calico covering picture and frame to reveal the bald, pear-shaped head, the staring, watery-blue fish-eyes and flabby cheeks of the old lady's late husband, the Lord High Chamberlain.

Although he had long since forgotten who had told him, Ottokar Vondrejc had heard from somewhere that the Count had been cruel and harsh, pitiless not only towards the sufferings of others, but also towards his own. It was said that as a child he had hammered a nail through his foot into the floor, merely to amuse himself!

The house was full of cats, all of them old, slow, creeping creatures. Often Ottokar would see a dozen or so walking up and down the corridor, grey and quiet, as if they were witnesses waiting to be called into court. They never entered the room; however, if, by mistake, one did put its head round the door, it would immediately withdraw it in haste, as if it quite agreed it was not time for it to give evidence yet.

Countess Zahradka's attitude to Ottokar was strange. Sometimes he would detect in her look something of the tender caress of a mother's love, but it would only last for a few seconds; the next moment he would feel a wave of icy contempt, almost hatred.

Her love, if it was that, was never expressed in words, but often enough her cruel arrogance found eloquent expression, even if it was more in the tone of what she said than in the actual meaning of her words.

He had first been commanded to perform before her on the occasion of his first communion, playing the Czech folk-song 'Andulko, mé dítě, já vás mám rád' on his half-size violin. Later he had played other tunes, love songs and hymns until, as his playing and technique improved, he could perform Beethoven sonatas; but never, no matter whether his performance was

good, bad or indifferent, had he seen the slightest sign of app-
roval or disapproval on her face. Even now, he had no idea
whether she appreciated his playing.

Sometimes he had tried to appeal to her emotions by impro-
vising, to see if he could sense, from the rapid fluctuations of her
response, whether his music had found the key to her heart; but
he often felt her love when he was playing out of tune, and hatred
when he reached the heights of virtuosity.

Perhaps the unbounded arrogance of her blood responded to
the perfection of his playing as to an intrusion on her aristocratic
privileges and flared up in hatred; perhaps it was her Slav
instinct only to love what was weak and feeble; perhaps it was
merely chance, but there was always an insurmountable barrier
between them, and he very soon gave up the idea of trying to
remove it, just as it never occurred to him to push past her to look
out of the windows.

He gave her a mute, respectful bow, opened his violin-case,
tucked his instrument under his chin and raised the bow to the
strings, which prompted her stock, offhand response, "Well
then, Pane Vondrejc, play your fiddle." Perhaps it was the contrast between the excitement he had felt as he stood outside
Wallenstein Palace and the feeling of being trapped in the past
which overcame him in this grey room, that led him, without
thinking, to play the silly, sentimental song from the days of his
first communion, 'Andulko ...'. As soon as he heard himself
play the first few notes, he started in confusion, but the Countess
looked neither surprised nor annoyed; she was merely staring
into space, like the portrait of her husband.

Gradually he began to improvise on the tune, following the
inspiration of the moment. He would regularly allow himself to
be carried away by his own playing, which he then listened to
in astonishment, as if it were another person playing, not
himself, but a different person who was inside him and yet not
himself, a person of whom he knew nothing except that he
guided the bow. Ottokar would be so carried away by his music
that the walls about him disappeared and he would find himself

wandering round a dreamworld filled with shimmering colours and sounds, where he plunged into uncharted depths and surfaced with mellifluous jewels. Then it would sometimes happen that the dull windows became crystal-clear, and he knew that beyond them was a glorious fairy realm, filled with the flutter of glistening white butterflies, living snowflakes in the middle of summer; and he would see himself walking down unending avenues of overarching jasmine, drunk with love, his spirit bathed with the scent from the skin of the young woman in bridal white whose warm shoulder was pressing in intimate embrace against his own.

Then, as so often happened, the grey linen masking the portrait of the dead Count would turn into a cascade of ash-blond hair beneath a sunny straw hat with a pale-blue ribbon, and he would see a girl's face with dark eyes and half-open lips gazing down at him.

Dreaming, waking, sleeping, he felt those features within him, as if they were his true heart; and every time he saw them come alive, the 'other person', who was inside him, seemed to obey a mysterious command, which came from 'her', and his music took on the dark tones of a wild, alien cruelty.

The door to the adjoining room was suddenly opened and the young girl who had been in his thoughts entered quietly.

Her face resembled the portrait of the young lady in the Rococo crinoline in Elsenwanger House, she was just as young and beautiful. Behind her a horde of cats peeked in.

Ottokar looked at her as calmly as if she had been there all the time. What was there to be surprised at? She had simply stepped out of his mind and appeared before him.

He played and played, self-absorbed, lost in his dreams. He saw himself standing with her in the deep darkness of the crypt of St. George's, the light from a candle carried by a monk flickering on a barely life-sized statue in black marble: the figure of a dead woman, half decayed, her dress in tatters over her breast, her eyes shrivelled and a snake with a horrible, flat, triangular head curled up inside her torn-open stomach in place of a child.

And the music of his violin changed into the words, as monotonous as a ghostly litany, which the monk in St. George's would repeat every day to visitors to the crypt:

"Many years ago, there was a sculptor in Prague who lived with his mistress without the blessing of the Church. And when he saw that she was with child, he no longer trusted her and, believing she had deceived him with another man, he strangled her and threw the body down into the Stag Moat. The worms had already gnawed at her when they found it. They locked the murderer in the crypt with the corpse and, as penance for his sin, compelled him to carve her likeness in stone before he was broken on the wheel."

All at once Ottokar came to, and his fingers stopped on the strings as his waking eye suddenly caught sight of the girl standing behind the old Countess' chair and smiling at him. He froze, incapable of movement, the bow raised in his hand.

Countess Zahradka took up her lorgnette and slowly turned her head. "Carry on playing, Ottokar. It's only my niece. Don't disturb him, Polyxena."

Ottokar did not move, only his arm fell loosely to his side, as if under the effect of a heart spasm.

For a good minute there was complete silence in the room.

"Why have you stopped playing?" asked the Countess angrily.

Ottokar pulled himself together, scarcely knowing how to hide the fact that his hands were trembling; then, softly, shyly, the violin began to whimper:

> "Andulko,
> My little child
> I do love you."

A purring laugh from Polyxena brought the melody to a halt. "Won't you tell us, Herr Ottokar, what that marvellous tune was that you were playing before? Was it an improvisation? It – called – up", after each word Polyxena paused meaningfully; her eyes were lowered, and she plucked at the fringes of the chair, apparently lost in thought, "a – vivid – picture of – St. George's – crypt, Herr ... Herr ... Ottokar."

The old Countess gave an almost imperceptible start. There was something about the tone in which her niece spoke the name Ottokar which aroused her suspicions.

The bewildered student stammered a few embarrassed words. There were two pairs of eyes fixed upon him, the one full of such consuming passion that they seemed to scorch his brain, the other penetrating, razor sharp, radiating suspicion and deadly hate at the same time. He could not look at either without either hurting the one deeply or revealing his innermost feelings to the other. 'Quick! Play! Just keep on playing!' screamed a voice inside him. Hastily he raised his bow. Beads of sweat were forming on his forehead. 'For God's sake, not that blasted 'Andulko' again!' As he drew the bow across the strings he felt to his horror that it was inescapable ... everything began to go black ... then the sound of a hurdy-gurdy from the street outside came to his rescue and, with crazed, mindless haste, he rushed into the music-hall song with the chorus:

> "Pale as the lily
> Never should marry,
> My mother said;
> Lips like the cherry,
> Rosy and merry,
> Kiss and soon wed."

After one verse, he stopped; the gust of hatred that came from Countess Zahradka almost knocked the bow out of his hand.

Through a veil of mist he saw Polyxena dart over to the grandfather clock by the door, pull the linen cover aside and push the finger round until it pointed to VIII. He realized it was a way of telling him the time for their rendezvous, but the joy

57

froze in his throat at the fear that the Countess might have seen through the stratagem.

He saw her long, skinny, old woman's fingers rummaging in the knitting bag hanging from the back of the chair and sensed that she was about to do something that would be unimaginably humiliating for him, something so terrible he dared not even guess what it might be.

"Capital – music – Vondrejc – capital", said the Countess, spitting out each word separately, took two crumpled notes from the bag and handed them to him. "There's – a tip – for you. And buy yourself – a pair of – better – trousers on my account before the next time, those are all worn and shiny."

Ottokar's heart almost stopped beating with the shame. His last clear thought was that he had to take the money, if he did not want to give himself away. Before his eyes the whole room dissolved into a cloud of grey: Polyxena, the clock, the face of the late Chamberlain, the suit of armour, the armchair, only the dusty windows stood out, whitish rectangles bursting through the gloom. He realised that the Countess had drawn her own grey cover over him – 'as a protection against the flies' – and that he would never be able to rid himself of it until death.

He found himself out in the street, with no memory of how he had come down the stairs. Had he been in the upstairs room at all? A burning wound deep within him told him that he must have been. And he was still clutching the money in his hand. Unthinking, he thrust it into his pocket.

Then he remembered that Polyxena would come to him at eight o'clock; he heard the towers strike the quarter; a dog yapped, it struck him like a whiplash across his face: Did he really look so shabby that the dogs of the rich barked at him?

He clenched his teeth together, as if he could grind his thoughts into silence, and raced on trembling legs towards his home. At the next corner he stopped, swaying to and fro. 'No, not home. Away, far away from Prague.' He was consumed with shame, 'The best would be to throw myself into the river!' With the decisiveness of youth he immediately set off for the

Moldau, but the 'other person' inside him slowed his steps, whispering that he would surely betray Polyxena, if he were to drown himself, and concealing from him the fact that it was the vital urge within that was holding him back from suicide.

'Oh God, my God, how can I look her in the face when she comes?' he sobbed to himself. 'No, no, she won't come, it's all over.' At that the pain in his breast sunk its fangs even more deeply into his soul: if she did not come to him any more, how could he go on living?

He went through the black and yellow striped gate into the courtyard of the Dalibor Tower, aware that the next hour would be an endless torment as he counted each minute. If Polyxena came he would shrivel before her with shame; if she did not come, then the night of madness would swallow him up.

He shuddered as he glanced over at the dungeon tower with its round, white hat, towering up from the Stag Moat behind the crumbling wall. He had a dim feeling that the tower was still alive: how many victims had already succumbed to madness in its stone belly, but still the Moloch was not satisfied; now, after a hundred years of death-like sleep, it was awakening again.

For the first time since his childhood he saw it not as the work of human hands, but as a granite monster with fearsome entrails that could digest flesh and blood, just like those of some nocturnal predator. It had three stories with a round hole down the middle like a pipe from gullet to stomach. In the dreadful darkness of the top floor, year after lightless year had gnawed at the condemned prisoners, until they were let down by ropes into the middle room for their last loaf of bread and jug of water, after which they would die of thirst, unless, crazed by the reek of decay from below, they flung themselves through the hole to join the stinking cadavers.

The courtyard of limes breathed the dewy damp of the evening twilight, but the window of the keeper's cottage still stood open. Ottokar sat down on the bench, as quietly as possible so as not to disturb the old, gout-ridden woman who, so he believed, was sleeping on the other side of the wall. He wanted to clear his mind of all that had happened for a moment, before the torture of waiting began: a childish attempt to outwit his heart.

He was suddenly overcome with a feeling of weakness; it needed all his strength to hold back the sobs which gripped him by the throat and threatened to suffocate him. From inside the room, he heard a toneless voice, which sounded as if someone were speaking into a pillow, "Ottokar?"

"Yes, mother?"

"Aren't you going to come in for your dinner?"

"No, mother. I'm not hungry; I – I've already had something to eat."

For a while the voice was silent.

In the room the clock chimed a soft, metallic half past seven. Ottokar pressed his lips together and clenched his hands. 'What should I do? What should I do?!'

Again he heard the voice. "Ottokar?"

He did not reply.

"Ottokar?"

"Yes, mother?"

"Why ... why are you crying, Ottokar?"

He gave a forced laugh. "Me? Whatever are you thinking, mother! I'm not crying. Why ever should I cry?"

The voice fell silent, unbelieving.

Ottokar raised his eyes from the shadow-dappled courtyard. 'If only the bells would finally ring out and break this deathly silence!'

He stared at a crimson gash in the sky, and felt that he had to say something.

"Is father in there?"

"He's at the inn", came the answer after a pause. He stood up quickly. "Then I'll go and join him for an hour or so. Goodnight, mother." He picked up his violin case and looked at the tower.

"Ottokar?'

"Yes? Should I close the window?"

"Ottokar! Ottokar, I know you're not going to the inn. You're going in the Tower, aren't you?"

"Yes ... well ... later. It ... it's the best place for practising. Goodnight."

"Is she coming to the Tower again tonight?"

"Božena? Who knows. She might. If she's free she sometimes comes and we have a chat. Is there any message for father?"

The voice became even sadder, "Do you think I don't know it's someone else? I can tell by her tread. No one who has been working hard all day would step so lightly and so quickly."

"You do get funny ideas, mother!" He tried to laugh.

"Well, I've said my piece. And you're right, you'd better close the window. It's better like that, then I won't be able to hear those awful songs you always play when she's with you. I ... I wish I could help you, Ottokar."

Ottokar held his hands over his ears, then he put the violin case under his arm, hurried across to the gap in the wall and ran up the crumbling stone steps and across the little wooden footbridge into the top floor of the Tower. The semicircular room where he was standing had a narrow window, really no more than an enlarged slit for bowmen to shoot through, in the three-foot-thick wall; it looked out to the south and in it the silhouette of the cathedral hovered over the ancient castle. For the visitors who came to visit the Dalibor Tower during the day there were a few rough wooden chairs, a table with a jug of water on it and an old, faded sofa. In the darkness, they looked as if they were rooted to the ground. A small iron door with a crucifix on it led into the adjoining chamber where, two hundred years ago, a Countess Lambua, Polyxena's great-great-grandmother, had been imprisoned. She had poisoned her husband and before she died, in her madness, she had bitten open the arteries of her wrist and painted his portrait in blood on the wall.

Behind it was a dark cell, scarcely six foot square, where, with a piece of iron, a prisoner had scratched a cavity in the stone blocks of the wall, deep enough for a man to squat inside. He had scraped away for thirty years; a handsbreadth more and he would have been free – free to throw himself into the Stag Moat below. But he had been discovered in time and moved to the middle of the tower, where he had starved to death.

Restless, Ottokar paced up and down, sat in the window, stood up again; one minute he was certain Polyxena would come, the next he was convinced he would never see her again; each possibility seemed more dreadful than the other, each contained his hopes and fears together.

Every night Polyxena's image accompanied him in his dreams, waking and sleeping it filled his life. He thought of her when he played the violin, when he was alone he held imaginary conversations with her. He had built the most fantastic castles in the air for her, but what did the future hold? In the boundless despair of youth, such as only a heart of nineteen years can feel, he saw it as an airless, lightless dungeon.

The idea that he might ever play on his violin again seemed an utter impossibility. There was a faint, scarcely audible voice inside him, telling him that everything would turn out quite differently from his imaginings, but he did not listen, refused to listen to it. Often pain can be so overpowering that comfort, even if it comes from within, only makes it burn all the more.

The gathering darkness in the deserted room only increased his agitation until it was unbearable. He kept on imagining he heard soft noises outside, and his heart stood still at the thought that it must be 'her'. Then he would count the seconds until, according to his calculation, she should have found her way in through the darkness, but every time his expectation was disappointed, and the thought that she might have turned back on the threshold drove him almost to distraction.

He had become acquainted with her only a few months ago. It seemed to him like a fairytale come true when he thought back to it. Two years before that he had seen her, but as a picture, as the portrait of a lady from the Rococo period with ash-blond hair, narrow, almost transparent cheeks and a strange, cruelly lascivious expression round her half-open lips, behind which glistened the white of tiny, bloodthirsty teeth. The picture hung in the portrait gallery of Elsenwanger House, and one evening, when he had been sent to play to the guests there, he had seen it looking down at him from that wall, and it had branded itself on his mind so that whenever he closed his eyes and thought of it, it appeared clearly before him. Gradually it had come to dominate his youthful yearning and so captured his whole being that it had eventually come to life, so that in the evenings, when he sat on the bench beneath the limes dreaming of her, he could feel it nestling against his breast like a creature of flesh and blood.

It was the portrait of a Countess Lambua, he had been told, and her first name was Polyxena.

From then on he invested that name with all the beauty, joy, glory, happiness and sensuality his youthful imagination could dream up, until it became a magic word, which he only needed to whisper for him to feel the presence of its bearer like a caress which scorched him to the marrow. In spite of his age, and the fact that until then he had enjoyed perfect health, he sensed that the heart condition that suddenly began to trouble him was incurable and that he was doomed to die young, a feeling that never filled him with sadness, but was more like a foretaste of the sweetness of death.

From his childhood on, the strange, unworldly setting of the Dalibor Tower with its gloomy stories and legends had encouraged him to build castles in the air, in contrast to which the world around, with its poverty and oppressive narrowness, seemed a hostile dungeon. It never occurred to him to try to connect his dreams and longings with his everyday reality. Time stretched ahead of him, empty of plans for the future.

He had had very little to do with children of his own age. For a long time his world had been bounded by the Dalibor Tower with its lonely courtyard, his taciturn foster-parents and the old tutor, who had taught him until well past childhood because the Countess, who paid for his upbringing, did not want him to attend school.

His cheerless existence, and his separation from the world of ambition, the race for fame and fortune, would probably have turned him, before his time, into one of those solitary eccentrics wrapped up in their own daydreams who were so common on the Hradschin, had not something happened which had turned his soul upside down, something so uncanny and yet at the same time so real, that with one blow it had demolished the wall separating his inner life from the world outside, turning him into a man who had moments of ecstasy in which even his wildest fantasies seemed within easy grasp.

It had happened in the cathedral. He was sitting among old women saying their rosaries; he had been staring at the tabernacle, oblivious to his surroundings, not noticing their comings and goings, until all at once he realised the church was empty apart from someone sitting beside him – the very image of Polyxena! It was the very same face he had been dreaming of all this time, right down to her delicately chiselled nostrils and the curve of her lips.

For a moment, the gap between dream and reality closed, but only for a moment; a second later he was fully aware that it was a living girl he could see beside him on the bench. But that single moment was enough to give fate the purchase it needs to prise a person's destiny for ever off its predetermined path of rational decision and to send it careering into that boundless world where faith can move mountains.

In the confused, sensual ecstasy of one who finds himself face to face with the idol of his yearning, he had flung his arms wide and thrown himself down before the physical incarnation of all his dreams, he had called out her name, embraced her knees, covered her hands with kisses; trembling with excitement, he had told her, in a tumbling cascade of words, what she meant to him, that he had known her for a long time, without ever having seen her in the flesh.

And there in the church, surrounded by the golden statues of the saints, they had both been seized by a wild, unnatural love, which had carried them away like a hellish whirlwind, raised by the sudden stirring of a ghostly line of depraved ancestors, who for centuries had been confined to the portrait gallery.

As if by some satanic miracle, the young girl, who entered

the cathedral an innocent virgin, had, by the time she left, also been transformed into the *spiritual* likeness of her ancestress, who had borne the same name of Polyxena and whose portrait now hung in Baron Elsenwanger's town house.

Since that day they had met whenever they had the opportunity, without prior arrangement and without ever not finding the other. It was as if there were some magic attraction in their passion that drew them together; they acted instinctively, like dumb animals on heat who do not need understanding, because they understand the call of the blood. Neither of them found it at all surprising when chance led to their paths crossing at the very moment when their lust for the other was at its strongest. For Ottokar, each time he saw that it was Polyxena, and not merely her image, in his arms, it was the constant renewal of a miracle, such as had been repeated but an hour ago.

When he heard her steps approaching the tower – this time it really was her – his torment had already disappeared, had faded away like the memory of some illness he had long since recovered from. When they were in each others' arms he was never sure whether she had come through the door, or through the wall, like some apparition. She was with him and that was all that he knew, or wanted to know; anything that had happened before had been swallowed up in the abyss of time.

And that was how it was now.

He saw her straw hat with the pale-blue ribbon appear in the darkness of the room, then it was thrown carelessly into a corner, and everything else followed; her white dress was like a cloud of mist on the table, the rest of her clothes were scattered around the chairs; he felt her hot skin, her teeth biting into his neck, heard her groans of pleasure: everything happened too quickly for him to grasp, like a series of lightning images, each one displacing the last, each one more overwhelming. He was in an ecstasy of voluptuousness which blotted out all sense of time. Had she asked him to play his violin for her? He had no idea, could not recall her saying so.

All he knew was that he was standing upright before her, her arms embracing his loins; he could feel Death sucking the blood from his veins, could feel his hair stand on end, his skin freeze, his knees tremble. He was incapable of rational thought, at times he felt he was about to fall backwards, then, at that very moment, he would wake, as if she were holding him up, and hear a song from the strings that his bow and his hand must have been playing, but that also came from her, from her soul and not from his, a song in which lascivious desire was mingled with fear and horror.

Half unconscious, unable to resist, he listened to the story the music told: everything Polyxena imagined, in order to whip herself up into an even greater frenzy of lust, he saw as a series of vivid images; he felt her thoughts pass into his mind, watched them come to life and then read them in elaborate letters on a stone slab: it was the extract from an old chronicle on which the picture 'The Man Impaled' was based, just as it is inscribed in the Little Chapel on the Hradschin, in memory of the gruesome end of one who tried to seize the crown of Bohemia:

'Now one of the knights who had been impaled went by the name of Bořivoj Chlaveć, and his stake had come out by the pit of his arm, leaving his head unharmed. This Sir Bořivoj prayed most fervently until the evening, and during the night his stake broke off at his backside and he went, with the rest of the stake still inside him, up to the Hradschin and lay down upon a dung-heap. In the morning he went straight to the house that stands beside the Church of St. Benedict and sent for a priest from the castle clergy, in whose presence he most fervently confessed his sins before the Lord our God and told him that without confession and receipt of the Holy Sacrament of one kind, as ordered by the Church, he could not die; it had been his custom every day to say a short prayer in honour of Almighty God and an Ave Maria in honour of the Blessed Virgin, and it had ever been his assurance that through the power of this prayer and the intercession of the Blessed Virgin he would never die without first receiving the sacrament of Holy Communion.

The priest spake, "My son, tell me that prayer", and he began, saying, "Almighty God, I beseech Thee, grant me the intercession of Thy most holy martyr, Saint Barbara, that I shall not die a speedy death but shall receive the Holy Sacrament before mine end, that, protected from all enemies, both visible and invisible, and preserved from evil spirits, I may at the last be brought to eternal life, through Jesus Christ our Lord and Saviour, amen."

After these words, the priest administered the Holy Sacrament, and he died the same day, and there was much wailing among the people when he was buried in the Church of St. Benedict.'

Polyxena had gone, and the tower lay lifeless and grey beneath the glittering stars of the night sky; but in its stony breast beat a tiny human heart that was full to bursting with the oath it had sworn not to rest and rather to share a thousandfold the cruel torture of the impaled knight than to die before he had laid at his lover's feet the highest prize that human will can aspire to.

Chapter Four

In the Mirror

For a whole week Dr. Thaddaeus Halberd had been unable to overcome his annoyance with himself. His visit to Lizzie the Czech had put him in a permanent bad mood, but the worst thing about it was that he could not get the memory of his love for her out of his mind.

He blamed the balmy spring air, whose narcotic effect seemed stronger than ever that year, and every morning he scrutinised the clear blue sky for some sign of a cloud to cool the late-flowering passion bubbling through his old veins.

Was it the goulash at Schnell's that was too peppery? he asked himself as he lay in bed, quite unable, contrary to his usual habit, to get to sleep. He kept on relighting his candle so that he could see the curtain over the window clearly; in the moonlight it kept taking on all sorts of grotesque, ghostly forms. To try to take his mind off Lizzie, he had had the bizarre idea of subscribing to a newspaper, but that only made things worse. Hardly had he found an article that interested him, than his eye was caught by a blank column, which did not even disappear when he put his pince-nez on over his spectacles. At first he was afraid this distressing phenomenon was the result of defective vision, which might even be caused by the initial stages of some mental illness, until his housekeeper solemnly assured him that she too could see the same blank spaces, at which he gradually came to the conclusion that they were merely the result of the censors' activity, to protect the public from misleading information.

In spite of that, he still found the patches of white in the middle of pages covered with carbolic-scented printer's ink disturbing. Precisely because, deep down inside, he was well aware that he was only reading the newspaper to take his mind off Lizzie, every time he was about to turn over he was struck by the fear that the next page might be completely blank and that instead of a patriotic leading article, the hideous features of the old courtesan might gradually form on the paper, as a kind of physical manifestation of his psychological worries.

He hardly dared go anywhere near his telescope. The very memory of the way the old woman had grinned at him through the lens still made his hair stand on end. Once or twice he did force himself to look through it, just to prove to himself that he had the courage, but it took a lot of clenching of his perfect false teeth before he could bring himself to take just a quick peep.

During the day his thoughts still kept going back to the actor, Zrcadlo, but he naturally rejected any suggestion that he might make a further attempt to visit him in the New World.

Once he had brought up the subject of the somnambulist with von Schirnding – it was at Schnell's, and the Baron was biting into a sow's ear pastry filled with horseradish cream – and had learnt that since that evening Konstantin Elsenwanger had been a changed man: he refused to see anyone at all, and lived in constant fear that the invisible document that Zrcadlo had placed in the drawer might after all turn out to be real and that his brother Bogumil might have disinherited him posthumously.

"And why not?" Baron von Schirnding had said, putting down his pastry in irritation. "If miracles can happen and people's faces can change under the influence of the moon, then why shouldn't the dead disinherit the living? Elsenwanger's quite right to leave the drawer closed without even looking to see. Better to be stupid than ruined."

Halberd had agreed with him, though only out of politeness. For his part, he found it impossible to keep the drawer in his mind which contained Zrcadlo closed; on the contrary, he lost no opportunity to rummage round inside it.

'I must pop into the Green Frog one evening, perhaps I'll see the fellow there', he resolved, when he was going over the matter once more. 'Lizzie – I can't get that damned woman out of my mind, she must be a witch – said he went round the inns.'

That very evening, just as he was about to go to bed, he decided to carry out his plan, rebuttoned the braces he had already started to undo, put his coat back on and, arranging his features in a forbidding expression (so that any slight acquaintances he might meet out that late would not entertain improper thoughts as to his intentions), set off down towards the Square of the Knights of St. John where, surrounded by venerable old palaces and monasteries, the Green Frog did nightly service to Bacchus.

Since the outbreak of war neither he nor his friends had been to the inn, but in spite of that the central room was still kept empty, reserved for the gentry, as if the landlord – an old gentleman with gold-rimmed spectacles and the kindly earnestness of a family lawyer whose only thought was to spend his every waking minute looking after the fortunes of his wards – had not dared to put it to any other use.

"What can I bring Your Ex'llency today?" asked the 'lawyer', his grey eyes lighting up with a friendly glow, after Halberd had taken his seat. "Aha, a bottle of Melniker. Red? 1914 vintage?"

Even before this, the landlord had whispered to his waiter to bring a bottle of 1914 Melniker, which the latter had held hidden behind his back and now placed on the table with ape-like agility. The two of them then bowed low before disappearing into the bowels of the Green Frog.

The Penguin was sitting at the head of a table covered in a white cloth in a long room with, on either side, a curtained opening leading off into the neighbouring rooms. There was a large mirror attached to the main door, through which he could observe what was going on in the other rooms. The large number of oil paintings on the walls, all of them representing the great and the good from different decades, testified to the loyalty of the landlord, Herr Wenzel Bzdinka – with the stress on the 'Bzd' – , at the same time giving the lie to those outrageous claims by certain loose tongues that he had been a pirate in his youth.

The Green Frog had a certain historical claim to fame, for it was said that it was there that the revolution had broken out in

1848 – whether as a direct result of the vinegary wine the land-lord of the time used to serve, or for another reason, was a constant subject of discussion among the regulars. But it all served to emphasise the achievement of Herr Wenzel Bzdinka in so far getting rid of the tavern's former dubious reputation – not only through the excellence of the drinks he served, but also by his personal respectability, which he did not loosen one iota, however late the hour – that even married women, accompanied, of course, by their husbands, would sometimes dine there.

Doctor Halberd sat, lost in thought, with his bottle of Melniker, the belly of which glinted ruby-red from the light of the electric lamp standing on the table. Whenever he looked up, he could see a second retired Physician to the Imperial Court sitting at the table, and every time he did so, it struck him how odd it was that his reflection drank with the left hand, whilst he used his right, and that his double, were he to throw his signet ring to it, could only wear it on the ring-finger of its right hand.

'There's a strange reversal there', Halberd thought to himself, 'which would be quite terrifying, if we were not used to it from earliest childhood. Now, let me see, where is it that this reversal takes place? Of course: at one, single, mathematical point. It's remarkable enough that so much more can happen in such a tiny point than in three-dimensional space itself.' He desisted from pursuing this train of thought any farther because of a vague feeling of dread that if he did so, and applied the law implicit within it to other areas, he might well come to the conclusion that human beings were incapable of doing anything of their own free will, that they were merely the instruments of some mysterious point deep within them.

In order to remove the possibility of any further temptation, he abruptly switched off the lamp, thus rendering his reflection invisible. It was immediately replaced by parts of the neighbouring rooms, now the one on the right, now the one on the left, depending on which way Halberd leant.

Both were empty.

In one was a sumptuously laid table with many chairs round it; the other was a small chamber in the baroque style containing nothing but a sofa with plump cushions and a curved table in front of it. He was filled with an inexpressible melancholy at the sight of this second room. A romantic assignation that had taken place there many, many years ago, and that he had completely forgotten, now flooded back into his memory, right down to the very last detail. He recalled that he had recorded the experience in his diary. But how could he have put it into brief, sober words? 'Was I such a dry stick in those days?' he asked himself sadly. 'Or do we only really become intimate with our own soul as we approach the grave?'

It was on that sofa he had first made love to the young, doe-eyed Lizzie. He cast an involuntary glance at the dull mirror, perhaps it still showed her image? But no, the mirror that preserves everything that is reflected in it was the one he bore within himself; the one on the door was faithless, unremembering glass.

She had had a posy of tea-roses at her waist ... all those years ago ... he suddenly smelt the aroma of the flowers as if they were there beside him.

Memories that come back to life are like ghosts: they emerge, as if from a tiny point, then swell until they suddenly take on a spatial presence of greater beauty and immediacy than they ever had before.

Where was the lace handkerchief that she had clenched between her teeth to stop herself crying out at the passion of his embrace? It had had her initials embroidered on it, L.K. – Liesel Kossut – , one of a dozen he had once given her. Suddenly he could remember where he had bought them and had the initials embroidered, he could see the shop.

'Why didn't I ask her to give it to me? As a memento. All that's left of it now is the memory, or' – he shuddered at the thought – 'it's mixed up with her other rags and tatters. And I'm sitting here, all alone with the past.' He looked away, so as not to see the sofa any more. 'What a cruel mirror this earth is! It makes the images it produces slowly turn ugly and wither before they disappear.'

The room with the sumptuous table reappeared. The 'lawyer' was going silently from one chair to another, viewing the arrangement from different points, like a painter, to make sure the overall impression was satisfactory; silently he gestured to the waiter where to put ice-buckets for the champagne.

Then laughter and voices were heard outside and a group of men came in, most of them wearing dinner jackets with carnations in their buttonholes. They were all fairly young men-about-town, presumably either on leave or doing essential work, apart from one, clearly their host, a portly, jovial fellow in his sixties in a ministerial frock coat and sponge-bag trousers, with a golden watch-chain hung with trinkets stretched across his ample corporation. The waiter gathered their hats, walking sticks and overcoats until he was loaded like a packhorse and almost disappeared under them. As a final touch, one of the gentlemen popped his top-hat on his head.

Then they were all silent for a while as they studied the menu. Mine host stood there with an ingratiating smile, rubbing his hands together as if he were trying to knead his deference into an invisible ball.

"Aha, Mockturtlesuppe", rasped one of the swells, his monocle falling out as his eye lit on a dish with an English name. "Gott strafe England! May God punish England for making fun of a poor sea-creature. I don't see why we can't have it in plain German, but I still think I'll take a bowl of your excellent Mockturtlesuppe."

"Must be cooked by ze Kitchener himself, some for me too", giggled another, and the rest whinnied with laughter.

"Dear friends, hrrmph ...", murmured the jovial old gentleman, then stood up, closed his eyes and pursed his lips to launch into a speech, shooting his cuffs to attract his audience's attention. "Dear friends, hrrmph ... hrrmph ...", but he got stuck on 'hrrmph, hrrmph' and finally sat down, speechless, but with visible signs of satisfaction at the way he had chosen to designate his table companions.

For a good half hour no more shafts of wit came to Halberd's ear: the gentlemen were fully occupied devouring the widest possible range of dishes. He saw the waiter, directed by mine host, wheel in a small, nickel-plated table with a grill, on which a leg of mutton was sizzling over a spirit-flame, watched the swell with the monocle carve the roast expertly, whilst growling to his friends that they were miserable curs who were only sitting upright because they were cowards who were afraid to assume their natural posture in such bright lighting.

The young dandy seemed to be regarded as an authority on anything connected with the gastronomic art; he ordered the most bizarre dishes imaginable – pineapple slices fried in dripping, strawberries with salt, gherkins in honey – higgledy-piggledy, just as they occurred to him; his rasping voice barked out his orders in a tone that brooked no dissent, and the deadly earnestness with which he brought out his little maxims to justify his choice – "On the strrroke of ten, harrrd-boiled eggs are the food forr gentlemen!" or "Drrripping is a delicacy which lubrrricates the vitals" – seemed so grotesquely comic that the Penguin could scarcely repress a smile.

The inimitable Austrian manner of approaching trivialities with deadly earnest, whilst dismissing matters of so-called moment as mere pedantry, which he saw in microcosm before him, conjured up episodes from his own youth in his mind's eye.

Although he had never taken part in such bouts of gluttony himself, he still felt that, despite all the contrasts, he had something fundamental in common with the group in the other room: gorging themselves like Junkers from the backwoods of Prussia and yet remaining Austrian aristocrats to the tips of their fingers; possessing knowledge and learning, but preferring to hide it behind a show of grotesque whimsy, rather than making a vulgar display of it like those know-all pedants who have never outgrown their school-days.

The banquet gradually degenerated into general drunkenness, but a drunkenness of an odd and extremely comic kind.

None of them bothered with the others, each lived in a little world of his own.

When he was well under the influence, the jovial old gentleman revealed to the waiter that he was Dr. Hyacinth Braunschild, chief steward of the estates of His Highness, Prince ... Hrrmph! He climbed up onto one of the chairs and, amid much bowing and scraping and tugging of his forelock, made a speech of homage to 'His Highness, his gracious patron, his Lord and Master' which consisted mainly of 'hrrmphs'. Each time he actually managed to complete a sentence, the swell with the monocle decorated him with the Ancient Order of the Smoke-Ring.

The only thing that stopped His Highness, Prince Hrrmph's chief steward from losing his balance and falling off the chair was the solicitude of mine host, who – like Siegfried in his cloak of invisibility at the court of King Gunther – stood behind him and made sure that gravity did not take too many liberties.

Another of the men was sitting on the ground, legs crossed like a fakir, staring fixedly at his own nose and balancing a champagne cork on the top of his head, clearly under the impression he was an Indian holy man. The one who had been sitting next to him at table had smeared the contents of a cream horn over his face and was doggedly trying to shave himself with the fruit knife and a pocket mirror.

A third had set up a long row of liqueur glasses filled with different-coloured liquids and, as he announced in a loud voice, was going through various Cabbalistic formulae to find out what was the proper order in which to drink them.

Yet another, without realising it, had his left foot in its patent-leather shoe stuck in an ice-filled champagne bucket and was juggling with as many of the plates as he could grab. When the last had shattered on the floor, he started singing the old student song:

> "A bri-hick or a stone
> Is seldom alone –

Their habits are very grega-arious.
A brick or a stone,
Found on its own,
Will be up to something nefa-a-arious."

Then they all, including the waiter, had to – or at least were
supposed to – join in the chorus:

"Mindless games are played here,
We play mindless games.
Mindless games are played here,
We play mindless games.
Mindless games ..."

It was a mystery to Halberd how Zrcadlo had suddenly
managed to appear, as if by magic, in the middle of this drunken
racket. The landlord had not noticed him either, so that his
frenzied gestures suggesting that the actor should disappear on
the spot were either too late or simply ignored, and he was
clearly unwilling to risk taking him by the collar and throwing
him out because then Dr. Braunschild would surely have fallen
off his perch and broken his neck before he had a chance to pay
his bill.

The 'fakir' was the first of the party to notice the strange
newcomer. He leapt up, staring at him in horror, convinced that
his Indian devotions had drawn some astral figure from the other
world who was about to wring his neck.

There was certainly something repellent about the actor's
appearance; he had no make-up on this time, so that his yellow
parchment skin looked even more waxen and his sunken eyes
like shrivelled black cherries.

Most of the party were too drunk to notice anything strange.
Prince Hrrmph's chief steward had so far lost his capacity for
surprise that he gave a beatific smile and, in the belief that a new
'dear friend' was about to honour the party with his presence,
clambered down from his chair to enfold the ghostly intruder in

a fraternal embrace.

Zrcadlo did not move a muscle as he approached. He seemed to be in a deep trance, as on that evening at Baron Elsenwanger's. Only when the princely steward had staggered up to him and, clearing his throat with his usual 'hrrmph, hrrmph', threw his arms wide and made to clutch him to his bosom, did the actor suddenly raise his head and direct a look full of hostility at him. What followed happened in a flash and was so surprising that, for a moment, Halberd assumed the mirror had deceived him.

In his drunken stupor, Braunschild had approached Zrcadlo with his eyes closed. When he opened them again, only a couple of feet from the actor's face, he found himself staring at a death-mask that looked so gruesome that even Dr. Halberd in the darkened room leapt up and stared at the mirror.

The sight of the twisted, corpse-like features struck the poor *bon vivant* like a blow between the eyes. He sobered up with a start, but the expression on his face was more than one of mere fright. His nostrils suddenly became sharp and thin, like those of someone who has just unwittingly inhaled ether, his jaw dropped slackly, the blood drained from his lips, which curled in a spasm, revealing his teeth, and his ashen cheeks, hollow as if he were sucking them in, had round, purple spots; the blood had even drained from the hand he stretched out to ward off evil. He waved his arms about wildly a few times, then, choking, collapsed to the floor.

As a doctor, as a former Physician to the Imperial Family even, Halberd realised immediately that there was nothing to be done for him; nevertheless, he would have gone to his aid, if it had not been for the general tumult. It took only a few seconds for his friends, all shouting at once, and the landlord to carry the body out; the chairs and tables were overturned and pools of red and foaming wine from the broken bottles were spreading over the floor.

For a moment the Penguin was uncertain what to do, he was still dazed from the scene, which had taken place right in front of his horrified eyes and yet had a spectral, unreal quality, since he had only seen it in the mirror. When his mind had cleared, his first thought was, 'Where is Zrcadlo?'

He turned on the electric light and jumped back with a start: the actor was right in front of him. Like a patch of darkness that had been left behind, he stood there in his black gown, motionless, apparently in a deep trance, just as when the drunken Braunschild had staggered towards him.

Halberd subjected him to a close scrutiny, coolly reminding himself that at any moment the man might assume some other, gruesome appearance. But nothing of the kind happened; he remained as motionless as an upright corpse.

"What do you want?" he asked in curt, imperious tones. All the time he was observing the veins in his neck, but he could see not the least sign of a pulse. "Who are you?"

No answer.

"What are you called?"

No answer.

Dr. Halberd thought for a moment, then lit a match and shone it in the sleepwalker's eyes. His pupils, scarcely distinguishable from the dark iris, remained dilated and did not react to the bright light at all. He took Zrcadlo's arm, which was hanging down loosely, and felt his wrist; his pulse – if he was not just imagining it – was so faint and slow that it was more like a distant echo of the languid pendulum of the clock on the wall than a sign of life. On-ne, two-o, three-ee, f-four. Fifteen beats per minute at the most.

Concentrating hard, Halberd went on counting and asked again, in a loud, piercing voice, "Who are you? Answer me!"

Then, all at once, the actor's pulse began to race and leapt from fifteen to a hundred and twenty. With a loud sniff, he drew in the air through his nostrils, and it was as if he had sucked in an invisible essence from the atmosphere around: his eyes suddenly shone and fixed on Halberd with an innocent smile. His whole attitude became soft and yielding, and his rigid features melted into an almost childlike expression.

At first Halberd believed the somnambulist had awoken to his true character, and asked in a friendly voice, "Now will you tell me who you really ..." but the words stuck in his throat. – That expression on the man's lips! Look, it was becoming clearer and clearer! And that face! That face! He was seized with the same feeling as at Elsenwanger's, only much clearer and more definite now: he knew that face, he had seen it so often. There was no possibility of doubt at all.

The memory came back slowly, very slowly, as if layer after layer were gradually being peeled away: he had once seen that face – perhaps it had been the very first time he had seen it – in some glittering object, a silver plate perhaps; at last he realised, with complete certainty, that that was the look he had as a child.

It was true that the skin, on which it appeared, was old and the hair above it grey, but the expression of youth, that indefinable something that no painter in the world can capture, shone through like a light.

"Who I am?" the words came from Zrcadlo's lips, but Halberd felt he was hearing his own youthful voice. It was a boy's voice and at the same time that of an old man, it had a strange double note, as if it came from two throats: the first came from far away in the past, the other, from the present, was like the echo from a sounding board that made the first loud and audible.

And the words themselves had a double note, a mixture of childlike innocence and the menacing earnestness of an old man.

"Who I am? Has there ever, since the beginning of time, been a man who knew the true answer to that question? I am the invisible nightingale that sits in its cage and sings. But it is not every cage whose bars resonate when it sings. How often did I sing to you, that you might hear me, but you have been deaf all your life long. There was nothing in the whole universe that was so close to you, so much a part of you, as I was, and now you are asking me who I am? Some people have become so estranged from their own soul that they fall down dead on the spot when the time comes for them to see it. They do not recognise it any

79

more; the face it shows them is the evil deeds they have done and which they have always feared might have stained their soul. You can only hear my song when you sing it as well. Anyone who cannot hear the song of his soul is guilty, guilty of a crime against life, against others and against himself. Innocent is the man who always hears the song of the nightingale, even if he should kill his father and mother."

"What is it I should hear? How can I hear it?" asked Halberd, completely forgetting, in his astonishment, that the man he was dealing with was not in his right mind, was perhaps even a madman. The actor ignored him and went on talking in his two voices which so strangely pervaded and complemented each other.

"My song is an eternal melody of joy. Anyone who does not know joy – that pure, unfounded, joyful certainty: I am that I am, that I was and ever will be – commits the sin against the Holy Ghost. The radiance of joy which shines in the breast, like the sun of an inner firmament, puts the ghosts of darkness to flight, those shades of forgotten misdeeds from earlier existences which follow men through their lives and twist the threads of their fate. Any who can hear the song of joy and sing it themselves will wipe out the effects of any guilt and will never more burden themselves with guilt.

If you are incapable of joy, the sun will die within you; how then can you spread light? Even an impure joy is closer to the light than dark, dreary earnestness.

You ask who I am? The innermost 'I' is the source of joy, and whoso does not worship it is a servant of hell. Is it not written, 'I' am the Lord thy God, thou shalt have no other Gods before me?

Anyone who does not hear the song of the nightingale and sing it, has lost his 'I', he has become a dead mirror where strange demons come and go, a wandering corpse, like the moon in the sky with its burnt-out fire.

Try to open yourself to joy.

There are many who try and who ask, 'What reason have I for

joy?' Joy needs no reason; like God, it grows of itself. Joy which needs a reason is not joy, but pleasure. Many who seek joy without finding it blame the world and fate. How could the first weak rays of a sun that has almost forgotten how to shine drive away the throng of ghosts from a thousand years of night? The crimes they have committed against themselves cannot be made good in one brief moment.

But once this pure, unfounded joy dwells within you, then you will have eternal life, for you will be united with your 'self' that knows not death, and you will have joy everlasting, even if you were born blind and crippled. But we must make the effort, we must long for joy; what most people long for is not joy, but the reason for joy."

'How strange', thought Halberd, 'he is a total stranger, I don't even know who he is or what he is, but my own self can speak to me through him. Has it left me and become *his* self? If that were the case, I would not be able to think myself. Can one live without a self?' He interrupted his train of thought, 'That's all nonsense, the wine must have gone to my head.'

His voice suddenly changing, Zrcadlo asked in a mocking tone, "You find that strange, Your Excellency?"

'Now I've got him!' thought Halberd grimly, forgetting the odd fact that the other had read his mind, 'now he's thrown off his mask.' But once more he was wrong.

Zrcadlo drew himself up, looked him straight in the eyes and stroked his smooth-shaven upper lip as if he had a long moustache, which he twirled at the ends and then pulled down.

It was a simple, unaffected movement, like a habitual gesture, but the effect was so convincing, that for a moment the bewildered Halberd imagined he really could see the moustache.

"You find that strange, Your Excellency? Do you seriously believe that any Tom, Dick or Harry you might meet in the street is in possession of his own self? On the contrary, all the time they are possessed by a ghost that plays the role of their selves. And have you, Your Excellency, not regularly found that your own self can be transferred to other people? Have you never noticed that people behave in an unfriendly manner towards you when you harbour unfriendly thoughts of them?"

"But the reason for that", objected Halberd, "might be that they can tell by your expression whether your thoughts are unfriendly or not."

"Aha." The spectre with the moustache gave a malevolent smile. "And a blind man? How about him? Can he tell from your expression?"

'He can tell from the tone of voice', Halberd was about to reply, but he suppressed his rejoinder because he felt in his heart that *the other was right*.

"You can reason everything away, Your Excellency, even with a mind that is not all that sharp and confuses cause and effect. Stop hiding your head in the sand. The behaviour of an ostrich is not what one would expect of a – penguin."

"Now you're being insolent!" Halberd was furious, but the spectre continued calmly,

"Better I am insolent than you should be, Your Excellency. Or do you not think it was insolent of you to use the microscope of science to try to penetrate the secret life of a 'sleepwalker'? Should you not like that, Your Excellency, please give me a good box on the ears, if it makes you feel any better, but do remember: it is not I you will be hitting, but poor old Zrcadlo. And that's the way it is with the 'self', more or less. If you should smash the electric lamp over there, do you think you would harm electricity? Just now you asked, or, rather, you *thought*, 'Has my self left me and passed to that actor?' And my answer is that the true self can only be recognised by its *effect*. It has no extension in space, and for that reason it is everywhere. Every-where. It is present everywhere.

You should not be surprised that your so-called *own* self should speak more clearly to you from another than from you yourself. Unfortunately, like almost all human beings, you have from your earliest days laboured under the misapprehension that your 'self' is your body, your voice, your mind or God knows what, and that is why you have not the slightest idea what

82

your 'self' is. The 'self' flows *through* people, and that is why we have to rethink our ideas before we can recognise our own 'selves'. Are you a Freemason, Your Excellency? No? Pity! If you were, you would know that in certain lodges the 'journeyman', when he is to become a 'master' has to enter the master's sanctuary *backwards*. And who does he find there? No one! If he were to find someone there, it would be another's, and not his own self. The *self* is the master. 'Am I talking to some invisible schoolmaster', you might ask, with a certain justification, Your Excellency, 'who instructs me without being asked?' Do not let that worry you; I am here because this is the right point in your life. For some people it never comes. By the way, I am not a schoolmaster. I am a Manchu."

"What are you?!" exclaimed Halberd.

"A Manchu. From the highlands of China. From the Middle Kingdom. As you might easily have guessed from my long moustache. This Middle Kingdom is to the east of the Hradschin. Even if you managed to bring yourself to cross the Moldau into Prague, it would still be a long, long way to 'Manchuria'.

But don't worry, I'm not dead, as you might perhaps suppose from the fact that I use Herr Zrcadlo's body as a mirror in which I appear to you. On the contrary, I am a 'living man'. There are several 'living men' beside me in the heart of the East. But don't make the mistake of hopping into your carriage and expecting your old grey nag to take you to the Middle Kingdom, to make my 'personal' acquaintance. The Middle Kingdom we inhabit is the kingdom of the *true* middle. It is the middle of the world, which is everywhere. In infinite space every point is a middle point. You do see what I am getting at?"

'Is he making fun of me?' wondered Halberd suspiciously. 'If he really is some kind of sage, why does he use expressions like 'hop into your carriage'?'

The ghost of a smile passed across the actor's face.

"Pomposity, Your Excellency, is the prerogative of buffoons. Anyone who cannot see the seriousness that lies beneath humour is also incapable of laughing at the false 'seriousness' of the cant which your respectable bourgeois imagines is forceful oratory; such a person is easily seduced by hypocritical enthusiasms and false ideals. The highest wisdom appears dressed as a clown. Why? Because once we have recognised something as 'dress', once we have seen through it, then it can only be a clown's costume, and anyone who is in possession of his self sees his own body – and those of others – as merely a clown's costume. Do you think the self could stand it here if the world really were the way it appears to humanity? You might object that everywhere you look is blood and horror. But where does that come from? I will tell you: Everything in the external world is based on the remarkable law of the plus and minus signs. It seems to many that it was the 'Good Lord' who created the world. Have you never asked yourself whether it might not have been a whim of the self? Since time immemorial there must always have been thousands on earth who wallowed in a feeling of – false! – humility. What is that other than masochism dressed in a cloak of sanctimony? That is what I call the 'minus signs', and if, in the course of time, they accumulate, they create a vacuum, sucking things in from the invisible realm. That arouses a bloodthirsty, savage, sadistic plus sign: a whirlwind of demons who use men's minds to unleash wars, slaughter and murder, just as I am using the mouth of this actor to give you, Your Excellency, a lecture.

Everyone is an instrument, only no one knows it. The self alone is not an instrument, it resides in the Middle Kingdom, far removed from plus and minus.

Every year, on April 30th, is Walpurgisnacht, the night when, people say, ghosts are released. There are also cosmic Walpurgisnachts, Your Excellency! They are too far apart in time for men to remember them, so that each time they are seen as a new, unique phenomenon.

Now is the point at which another such cosmic Walpurgisnacht is about to fall.

Everything will be turned upside down. One event will

explode upon another, almost without cause. Things will no longer be 'psychologically motivated', as they are in certain novels which make the problem of sex, decently clothed so that it can appear with even greater indecency, the key to life, and in which everything is resolved by the marriage of a respectable girl with no dowry.

The time has returned when the hounds of the Great Huntsman will break their chains, but something has been broken for us as well: the vow of silence!

We can speak!

That alone is the reason why I am talking to Your Excellency. It is the dictate of the moment and nothing to do with you personally. The time has come when the self is to speak to many.

There will be many who will not understand my speech. They will feel unrest inside them, such as a deaf person might feel when they sense someone is talking to them, but do not know what he wants. Such people will be deluded into thinking there is some deed they must carry out which in truth is not the will of the self, but the command of the fiendish 'plus-sign' in the bloody sky of the cosmic Walpurgisnacht.

What I have been telling Your Excellency was transmitted from a magic picture that was merely reflected in Zrcadlo; the words themselves came from the Middle Kingdom, from the self that is everywhere.

Your Excellency's honourable ancestors have for a thousand years cared for the physical health of the imperial house; how would it be if Your Excellency should concern yourself a little with the health of their souls?

I'm afraid I have to admit that until now you have not flown very high, Your Excellency. Schnell's and its goulash is not as close to the Middle Kingdom as one would wish. Rudimentary wings you have, of that there is no doubt (and what happens to those who have none at all you can see from what happened to our poor estate steward just now), otherwise I would not have troubled to appear to you. They're not true wings yet, as I said, but rudimentary wings, like – a penguin."

The ghost with the Tartar moustache was interrupted by the sound of the door-knob. As the door slowly opened, the room and everything in it passed across the surface of the mirror, as if every object in it had become detached. A policeman entered: "Excuse me, gentlemen, but it's twelve o'clock. It's closing time."

Before Halberd could ask any of the questions that were thronging his mind, Zrcadlo had silently disappeared.

Chapter Five

Aweysha

Every year on the 16th of May the feast of Bohemia's patron saint, St. John Nepomuk, was celebrated in Elsenwanger House with a huge meal held on the ground floor for the servants at which, following the age-old custom of the Hradschin, the master of the house in person sat at the head of the table.

On that night, beginning on the dot of eight and ending with the last stroke of midnight, all distinctions of rank between master and servant were suspended, everyone ate and drank together, shook hands and addressed each other by the familiar 'Du'.

The noble families were sometimes represented by one of their sons; if there were no sons, the duty devolved on the eldest daughter. Since his experience with Zrcadlo, Baron Elsenwanger had felt so exhausted that he had to ask his great-niece Polyxena, the young Countess Lambua, to take his place.

"Y'know, Xenerl", he had said to her, sitting by his desk in the library (surrounded by countless books, of which he had never opened a single one in his whole life), knitting a sock and holding the needles dangerously close to the candle whenever he thought he might have dropped a stitch, "Y'know, Xenerl, I thought, well, you're as good as a daughter to me, and they've all been with me for donkey's years. And if you want to sleep here afterwards and not bother going home so late at night, there's always the guest room, isn't there?"

Polyxena gave an absent-minded smile and, merely to have something to say, was about to tell him that she had already had her bed made up in the picture gallery when she remembered, just in time, what her nervous uncle's response to that was likely to be.

They must have sat for a good half hour in silence in the darkening room, Elsenwanger in his winged chair, a skein of yellow wool at his feet, giving a tortured sigh every few minutes, as if his heart were breaking, and Polyxena leaning back in a rocking chair beneath yellowing tomes, smoking a cigarette and half mesmerised by the soft, monotonous click of his knitting needles. Then she saw his hands suddenly stop and the knitting drop into his lap; a moment later his head nodded as he fell into the death-like sleep of old age.

As if she were under a spell, she was held in her chair by a strange weariness compounded of physical exhaustion and the feeling that she was being consumed from within by something for which she had no name. She was already leaning forward to stand up – 'perhaps it would be better if I opened the window and let in the cool, moist air?' – when the thought that it might wake her uncle, who would start some tedious old man's conversation with her, made her slump back down again.

She looked round the room that was now illuminated by the faint light of the candle alone. Covering the floor was a dark-red carpet with a boring pattern of garlands; she knew every twist and twirl by heart, so often had she played on it as a child. Even now she was choking on the smell of stale dust it gave off which – how many, many times! – had brought her to tears and blighted her young days.

And the eternal cries of, "Xenerl, be careful you don't make any nasty marks on your nice dress!" had been like grey clouds darkening the clear skies of childhood. The hatred she still felt made her clench her teeth on her cigarette, and she threw it across the room.

Now, when she looked back on it, her childhood seemed like a constant to and fro between equally dreary places. The sight of the long rows of mildewed volumes, which she had so often leafed through in the vain hope of finding a picture in them, were a painful reminder of those days. She had been like a nestling songbird trapped in some old ruin and desperately fluttering around in search of a drop of water: one week at home in Aunt Zahradka's gloomy castle, an excruciating Sunday here, then back home again.

She gave her old uncle a long, pensive stare. His crinkled, bloodless eyelids were so tightly closed that she could not imagine him ever opening them again. And she suddenly realised what it was about him – about him and her aunt – that she had so hated, even though neither of them had ever said a harsh word to her: the sight of their faces when they were asleep. It all went back to an apparently trivial incident from her earliest childhood:

She had been sleeping in her cot, scarcely four years old, and had suddenly woken up – perhaps she had had a fever, perhaps it had been a terrifying nightmare; she had screamed, but no one had come; she sat up, and there was her aunt on a chair, fast asleep in the middle of the room, and in such a deep, unconscious sleep that no shouts or cries could waken her. The shadows of her spectacles round her eyes had given her the look of a dead eagle and the petrified expression on her face had been one of pitiless cruelty.

From then on an aversion had formed in her child's mind to anything at all resembling the image of death. Initially, and for a long time, it was nothing more than a vague fear of sleeping faces, but later on it grew into a dull, instinctive hatred of anything drained of blood, of anything dead. This hatred had rooted itself all the more deeply within her, since her heart was full of a lust for life which had been suppressed for generations and was only waiting for an opportunity to blaze up and set her whole being on fire.

She had been surrounded by senility for as long as she could remember, by senile bodies and minds, senile in the way they spoke and behaved and in everything they did; the walls were covered with pictures of old men and women, and the whole city outside seemed senile, wrinkled, decrepit; even the moss on the ancient trees in the garden was like an old man's grey beard.

Then had come her school-days in the Convent of Sacré Coeur. At first the change in surroundings had brightened up her life, but only for a few brief days, before the light paled and darkened, became much too calm and solemn, too much like a weary sunset. The predator in her soul had crouched, waiting for the opportunity to pounce.

It was in the convent that she had heard the word 'love' for the first time: love of the Saviour, whom Polyxena saw constantly in her mind's eye, nailed to the cross, with the bloody marks, the bleeding wound in his breast and the blood dripping from the crown of thorns; love of prayer, in which the images she saw in her mind were transformed into words: blood, martyrdom, scourging, crucifixion, blood, blood; then the love for the Sacred Heart transfixed by seven swords. Candles in blood-red bowls. Blood. Blood.

Blood as the symbol of life etched itself on her soul.

Of all the aristocratic girls who were educated at Sacré Coeur, she was soon the most passionate.

But also passionate in ways she did not yet realise.

She scarcely understood the little French they were taught, the little English, the music and history and arithmetic and all the rest. She forgot it all immediately.

The only thing that stuck was love.

But it was love of ... blood.

It was long before she met Ottokar that she returned home from the convent, and as she felt the atmosphere of senility envelop her once more, the thing that had, during her years at school, been the object of her passionate love – the Saviour's martyrdom – seemed to sink slowly into a past that was a thousand years older than her tomb-like surroundings. All that was left was the lifeblood that flowed constantly from the 'other side', from the time of the crucifixion, through to her, a thin, oozing trickle of red.

And everything that she saw, that was lively and young, she subconsciously associated with the idea of blood. Everything that attracted her and filled her with longing – flowers, animals at play, a surge of joy, sunlight, young people, sweet scents and melodious sounds – resonated in the word that sounded in her soul, though she was only vaguely aware of it, like a dream in the uneasy sleep that precedes wakening: blood, blood, blood.

90

Then one day, when Baron Elsenwanger was giving a banquet, the room was unlocked where the portrait of her great-great-grandmother, Countess Polyxena Lambua, hung on the wall. When she saw it, among all the others, most of whom were also her ancestors, she had a strange feeling that it was not a picture of a dead person, but the reflection of a being that really existed somewhere, and was much more alive than anything she had ever seen. She had tried to persuade herself to ignore the feeling, but it kept on returning. 'It hangs there, surrounded by dead faces; it must be the similarity to my own fate that makes me respond to it', she told herself, without really believing it.

But that was not the reason. It was something else, something that was beyond her comprehension.

In a way, the picture on the wall was Polyxena herself. Just as the seed bears within it the image of the plant it will one day become, hidden to our sight and yet there in every organic detail, so the picture had been inside her from her earliest childhood, it was the predestined matrix into which her being was to pour every fibre and every cell, until she had filled out the very last recesses of the design.

What had made her feel that the portrait of her ancestress was more alive than anything she had ever seen, was the sudden, subconscious awareness it aroused within her of having seen herself, with all her characteristics, those that had unfolded as well as those that were still concealed within the bud.

The only thing that a person can feel is more alive than anything else in the world is that person himself.

She did not know the law, that is at the root of all magic: "If each of two quantities is equal to the other, then they are one and the same and only occur once, even if their existence appears to be separated by time and space."

Had she known it and understood it, she would have been capable of foreseeing her destiny down to the very last detail.

The portrait had its effect on her, just as it later did on Ottokar, only she was not pursued by it; she gradually merged with it and became it herself. Had she not been there, as the picture's living representative on earth, it would never have had the power to cast its spell over him. But now it was charged with the magic power of her blood, and his blood scented the presence of a living being and felt irresistibly drawn to it.

Then when Polyxena met Ottokar in the cathedral, no power in the world could have prevented what happened from happening. It was the inflexible law of destiny bringing to fruition what had been sown before. The seed had brought forth its fruit, the design that had been implanted in the body had ripened into deed, that was all.

The following day she had gone straight to confession, with the warning that had been drilled into her in the convent clear in her mind: that she would fall down dead if she held back a sin. But the blood had triumphed within her, and her conscience was silenced by the innocence of the sage and the innocence of the animal, who never feel remorse for any act they have committed. She was sure in her heart that she would not confess and that she would live. And in that she was right, and yet she was wrong. What, until that time, had seemed to be her self, had dropped down dead, but another 'self' – the one that corresponded to the picture of her ancestress – had instantly taken its place.

It is not mere chance that men call the succession of generations their family 'tree', for indeed, it is a tree which, after the long sleep of winter and the changing colour of its leaves, repeatedly puts forth the same branches.

The dead Polyxena in the portrait gallery had come to life and the living Polyxena had dropped down dead, they swapped places, and each one kept her innocence: the one refused to confess the sin the other had been compelled to commit. And each new day drew new buds from the young branch on the old tree, new and yet age-old, for they were the buds the family 'tree' had put forth from time immemorial.

And in Polyxena's mind love and blood coalesced into a single, indivisible idea. Driven on by the prickle of twisted desire – which her senile relations took for a rather overenthusiastic interest in history – she wandered round the Hradschin, from one place where blood had been spilt to another. Every grey, weatherbeaten stone, which beforehand she had ignored, had a story to tell of torture and murder, every foot of earth reeked of blood. When she touched the iron ring on the chapel door that King Wenceslas had clung to before his brother struck him down, she felt her body quiver at the mortal dread that still stuck to the metal, but which, within her, was transformed into wild, feverish lust.

The whole of the Hradschin with its mute, ossified buildings, had become a mouth that whispered stories of terror and horror from its past into her eager ear with a hundred living tongues.

Mechanically, Polyxena counted the strokes of the bells from the towers and spires announcing the eighth hour, then went down the stairs to the servants' dining room.

An old servant in a striped jacket came up to her, kissed her on both cheeks and led her to her seat at the head of a long oak table without a cloth.

Opposite her, at the lower end of the table, sat Prince Lobkowitz' coachman, a young Russian with a gloomy face and deep-set black eyes, who was one of several servants from other aristocratic houses who had been invited as guests; beside her sat a Tartar from the steppes of Kirgisia, with a round, red, fez-like cap on his smooth-shaven head. Someone told her he was Prince Rohan's groom and had served as guide to the famous Asian explorer, Csoma de Körös.

It was Božena, in her Sunday best, with her hair done up and crowned with an old toque with a nodding feather, a Christmas present from Countess Zahradka, who brought in the dishes: first of all partridge with sauerkraut, then sliced dumplings made from brown flour with *powidl*, prune jam.

"Enjoy it Polyxena", said Elsenwanger's old cook, "eat up and drink up", and she winked at the young housemaid who was huddling up close to her, as if she were a mother hen who would take her under her wing, if it should occur to the noble falcon at the head of the table to swoop down on her, claws outstretched.

At first the mood of the twenty or so men and women of varying ages was rather reserved; for some of them, the custom of sitting at table with one of their employers was new, and they were afraid of being clumsy with the knives and forks, but Polyxena quickly put them at their ease, starting conversations now with one, now with another, until they all joined in.

Only Molla Osman, the Tartar, sat in silence, eating his food with his fingers, which he kept rinsing in a bowl of water; and the gloomy Russian said not a word either, but just shot her occasional penetrating, almost hostile glances.

"But tell me", she said, when the table had been cleared and they had filled their glasses from the carafes of wine or the samovar, "what actually happened then. Is it really true that a somnambulist ...?"

"Indeed it is, your Ladyship", Božena replied eagerly, gasping at the dig in the ribs from the cook and quickly changing to the required familiarity. "True 'tis, Polyxena, I saw it with me own eyes. Terrible it was! I knew, the moment Brock started that howling and when the Baron said 'Jayzusjosephandmary!' And then his hands went all fluttery and he went flying round and round like a ... like a great big fiery cockerel with the blazing eyes that was on him. Thank God I had me little imp", she clutched an amulet she wore round her neck, "or I would've been cold stone dead from the wild look in his eye. Then he shot out over the box hedge, jako ... jako z rouru, like through a tube, and floated down to the ground. Pan Loukota", she turned to the ancient valet, "was a witness." "Rubbish", murmured the old man, shaking his head vigorously, "that wasn't the way of it at all."

"There you go, Pane Loukota", said Božena indignantly, "you'll be saying I'm not a reliable witness again, I'll warrant. But you were just as afraid as everyone else."

"What? He floated though the air?" asked Polyxena in disbelief.

"Ano, prosím ... yes, if you please."

"Really floated?"

"Prosím."

"And he had blazing eyes?"

"Prosím."

"And then, when he was with my aunt and my great-uncle and the other gentlemen, he is supposed to have changed his shape, or something?"

"Ano, prosím, he went tall and thin, like a broomstick", Božena assured her. "I saw it through the keyhole ..." she paused in embarrassment, aware that she had given herself away, "... but that was all I saw. I wasn't there 'cause her Ladyship your aunt sent me to fetch Lizzie the Czech ..." another dig in the ribs from Cook brought her tale to a complete halt.

For a while everyone was silent.

"This man – what is his name?" the Russian asked his neighbour in a low voice, but he just shrugged his shoulders.

"Zrcadlo, as far as I know", Polyxena answered instead. "I assume he's some kind of strolling player from the *Fidlowacka*, the fairground."

"Yes, that's what they said he was called."

"You think he has a different name?"

The Russian hesitated, "I ... I don't know."

"But he's some kind of actor, isn't he?"

"No. Definitely not." It was the Tartar who spoke.

"You know him? – You know him, Pane Molla?" they all cried out at once.

The Tartar waved away the suggestion. "I have only spoken to him once, but I believe I am not mistaken in my belief that he is the instrument of an evli." The servants stared at him, uncomprehending. When Polyxena asked him to explain, he thought for a moment, silently translating some words from his mother tongue into German, then said, "I know that it is something you do not have here in Bohemia, but in the East it is not that uncommon. An evli is a fakir magician who cannot speak without a mouth, so he speaks through the mouth of a dead man."

"You think Zrcadlo is a dead man?" the Russian asked, with

signs of great agitation.

"I do not know. Perhaps he is one of the not ... what is the word? ... the not ... no, the undead."

"One of the undead?"

"Yes. When the evli wants to speak through the mouth of another he first of all leaves his own body and enters that of the other. This is how he does it." The Tartar thought for a few moments, working out how to explain it. Then he placed his finger on his chest, above the diaphragm, at the point where the ribs join onto the breastbone. "This is the seat of the soul, which he draws up" – he pointed to his throat and then to the bridge of his nose – "first to here and then here. Then he leaves his body by breathing out, and enters the dead man; through his nose, then his neck and into his breast. If the corpse has not been damaged, the dead man will rise up and come back to life: but it is the evli."

"And what happens to the evli himself, while this is going on?" asked Polyxena, gripped with excitement.

"The evli's body appears dead as long as his soul is in the other. I have often seen fakirs and shamans, they always sit as if they were dead; that is because their spirit is in someone else. The name for this is 'aweysha'. But a fakir can also perform aweysha on living people, only they must be asleep or in a trance when he enters them. Some, in particular the dead who had very strong will-power when they were alive, or who still have a mission on earth to fulfil, can even enter living people while they are *awake*, without them noticing, but usually they also use the bodies of the undead or sleepers, such as Zrcadlo, for example. Why are you looking at me like that, Sergei?"

"Nothing, Molla, nothing; it's astonishing."

"At home", the Tartar continued, "it often happens that people who have lived quiet lives, suddenly forget what they are called and wander off. Then we say that an evli or a shaman has taken over their bodies. The shamans are unbelievers, but they have the same powers as the evliah; performing aweysha has nothing to do with the Koran. If we wake up in the morning with the feeling that we are not quite the same as when we went to sleep the night before, then we fear a dead soul might have entered us, and we breathe out vigorously a few times to free ourselves of it."

"But why is it that the dead want to enter the bodies of the living, do you think?" asked Polyxena.

"Perhaps for pleasure; perhaps to do something they left undone on earth; or, if they are cruel, perhaps it is to cause a great bloodbath."

"Then it could be that the war ..."

"Certainly", agreed Osman. "Everything that people do against their will comes from aweysha. If people suddenly start attacking each other like tigers, do you think they would do it if someone had not performed aweysha on them?"

"But surely they do it because ... well, because they believe in something, they are filled with fervour for it; for an idea perhaps."

"Yes, but that is aweysha."

"You mean fervour and aweysha are the same thing?'

"No. Aweysha comes first, and that creates the fervour. Usually people do not notice when an evli has performed aweysha on them, but they do notice the fervour, and therefore they assume it arose independently within them. There are different kinds of aweysha, you know. There are some who perform aweysha on others merely by holding a speech, that is aweysha too, even if of a more natural kind. But no one in the world can perform aweysha on a person who is completely self-reliant, not even an evli or a shaman."

"So you think the war started because some evli performed aweysha on us?"

Osman smiled and shook his head.

"Or a shaman?"

Again he shook his head.

"But who then?"

Molla Osman shrugged his shoulders. Polyxena could tell he did not want to say any more. His answer was an evasion. "No one can perform aweysha with someone who believes in himself and thinks before he acts."

"You are a Mohammedan?"

"N-no, not quite. As you can see, I drink wine." He raised his glass and drank to her.

Polyxena leant back and silently studied his calm features: a round, smooth face free of all passion or emotion. "Aweysha? What a strange superstition!" She sipped her tea. 'What would he say, I wonder, if I asked him if pictures can perform aweysha? Stuff and nonsense! He's nothing but a common groom.' She was annoyed with herself for listening to him for so long, and her annoyance only increased as she realised that she had never had a conversation with any of her relatives that was anywhere near as interesting; she felt it was an insult to her family. She half closed her eyes so that he would not see that she was observing him all the time. 'If I had him in my power, I would have his head cut off', she thought, trying to talk herself into a frenzy of blood-lust to bolster up her injured pride, but without success. She found it impossible to feel cruelty alone, it had to be coupled with love or lust, and both of those bounced off the Tartar as if he bore an invisible shield.

She looked up. During her conversation with Osman some of the younger servants had gathered at the end of the long room and were talking in low but excited voices. A few words came to her, "Proletariat ... nothing to lose ... chains." It was the servant, whom the Russian had earlier given a significant look, who was speaking. He was a young man with a vacant expression on his face, clearly a Prague Czech, who was showing off his reading and scattering socialist slogans around, "Property is theft."

Then there was a long muttering in which the name 'Jan Žižka' kept being repeated. "But that's all insane nonsense", hissed another, only with difficulty keeping his voice down. As if to relieve his irritation, he spun round on his heel, saying, "We'll be shot to pieces at the slightest protest. Machine guns! Ma-chine-guns!" But whatever he said, it had no effect, the Russian seemed to have an answer to everything. There was a

98

constant refrain of "Jan Žižka".

Suddenly the name "Ottokar Vondrejc" was mentioned. Polyxena heard it clearly; it froze her to the marrow. She instinctively leant forward to hear what was being said. The Russian noticed the movement and quickly signalled to the others, at which they immediately interrupted their discussion and made their way back to their seats as casually as possible.

'What was that all about?' wondered Polyxena. She instinctively felt it was directed against her and her caste. 'They would never have been so worked up if it had merely been dissatisfaction at their wages or something like that.'

What made her most uneasy was the fact that Ottokar's name had been mentioned. 'Do they know something?' She forced herself to reject the idea. 'Cowardly scum! What do I care? Let them think what they like. I will do as I please.'

She tried to read the expression on Božena's face. She knew that Ottokar and Božena had been lovers, but it had never concerned her. She was far too proud and arrogant to be jealous of a serving wench. No, Božena still looked friendly and unconcerned. Ottokar's name must have been mentioned in some other connection.

The barely restrained hatred in the eyes of the Russian coachman told her that it must have been something that went beyond personal matters.

She suddenly recalled a conversation she had heard by chance a few days before in a shop. There was the usual unrest down in Prague, someone had said. Yes, the mob were planning another of their 'demonstrations'. They would probably go round breaking windows, or taking part in other such 'democratic' activities.

She gave a sigh of relief. If that was all it was, what did it concern her? An uprising in Prague, a matter of no great consequence. So far that kind of thing had never crossed the bridges and approached the Hradschin. Those animals didn't dare attack the aristocracy.

She returned the Russian's stare with a cold, mocking look,

and yet a shiver still ran down her spine, so clear was the feeling of hatred he exuded.

But the shiver did not lead to fear; it was a thrill, a kind of voluptuous horror at the scenes she saw with her mind's eye if it should ever come to bloodshed. 'Ground-water' – in the middle of her thoughts the word 'ground-water' suddenly appeared. A voice within her seemed to have called it out. 'Why ground-water?' What connection did it have with the things she was thinking of? She was not even sure what ground-water was: something asleep in the earth? Asleep until it suddenly started to rise, to rise and rise until it flooded the cellars, undermined the walls, causing old houses to collapse overnight.

And an image rose from this subconscious idea: it was blood, rising from the depths, seeping up from the ground, pouring up out of the gratings over the drains, filling the streets until it flowed down into the Moldau.

Blood, the true ground-water of Prague.

She fell into a kind of trance. There was a red mist before her eyes. She saw it float slowly away from her towards the Russian, who went pale, choking with fear. She felt it was some kind of victory over the man. Her blood had been stronger than his.

'There is something in this ... this aweysha business, after all.' She looked at the Russian's hands: monstrous paws, broad, terrible, made for throttling – now they were lying on the table, paralysed, harmless.

A mocking voice rang out inside her, 'The hour is still far away when you proletarians can break your chains.' She suddenly knew that she could perform 'aweysha' if she wanted, perhaps had always been able to do so, for centuries, she and her family.

Chapter Six

Jan Žižka of Trocnov

On the last stroke of twelve the servants had stood up respectfully: the hour of equality was over.

Polyxena was in the picture gallery, uncertain as to whether she should make Božena help her undress. Then she dismissed her.

"Good night, your Ladyship", the girl took her sleeve and kissed it.

"Good night, Božena, off you go."

Polyxena sat on the edge of the bed, staring at the candle flame.

'Go to bed now?' the idea was unbearable. She went over to the arched window that gave onto the garden and drew back the heavy curtains. The moon was a thin, gleaming sickle hanging over the trees in a vain struggle against the darkness. The gravel path to the gate was faintly illuminated by the light from the downstairs windows. Formless shadows slipped across it, gathered, separated, swelled, disappeared, returned, lengthened, stretched long necks over the dark patches of grass, stood for a while like shapes of black mist among the bushes, shrank and then put their heads together, as if they had discovered some mystery that they had to whisper to each other in inaudible voices: the silhouettes of the figures down below in the servants' hall.

Immediately beyond the dark, massive park wall, as if the world came to an end at that point, a starless sky rose from cloudy depths, a gaping, immeasurable void.

Polyxena tried to deduce from the movements of the shadows what was being discussed down below, but in vain.

Was Ottokar already asleep?

She felt a soft yearning come over her, but only for a moment, then it was gone again. Her dreams were different from his, wilder, more passionate. Gentle fantasies could not hold her for long; she was not even sure that she really loved him.

What would happen if she were separated from him? She had occasionally thought about it, but never found an answer. It had been as pointless as her attempt just now to guess what the shadows were saying to each other.

To Polyxena, her own inner being was an unfathomable void, as impenetrable as the darkness outside. She was incapable of feeling sorrow, even when she imagined to herself that Ottokar had died that very moment. She knew that he had a weak heart and that his life hung by a thin thread, but when he told her, it was as if he had been talking to a picture, 'Yes' – she turned round – 'as if he had been talking to that picture on the wall there.'

She avoided the eyes of her ancestress, took the candle and went from one portrait to another: nothing but dead faces. None of them spoke to her. 'Even if they were to come to life before me, they would still mean nothing to me, I have nothing in common with them. They have turned to dust in their graves.'

Her eye was caught by the white of the turned-down sheet on her bed. 'Lie down and go to sleep?' She could not contemplate the thought. 'I think I would never wake up again.' Her uncle's sleeping face with its bloodless, tightly shut eyelids appeared before her. 'Sleep is something horrible, perhaps even more horrible than death.' She shuddered. The white bed-linen was like a shroud telling her how easily dreamless sleep could slip over into the eternal death of the mind. She was gripped with panic. 'For the love of God, I must get out, out of this room full of corpses! That page over there – so young and already decayed, his veins empty of blood, his hair on the floor of the coffin beside him where it fell from the grinning death's head. Old bodies, decayed in the vault. Old men, old women, I must get away from them all.'

She gave a sigh of relief when she heard a door open below and steps crunching across the gravel. She heard the soft murmurs of the servants saying goodbye and, blowing out the candle so she would not be seen from below, quietly opened the window and listened.

The Russian coachman stood in the gateway while the others disappeared, searching his pockets for matches. Then he lit a cigar. He seemed to be waiting for someone, Polyxena could tell by the furtive way he shrank back into the shadow whenever a noise came from the house, then peered out through the bars of the gate when it was quiet again. Eventually, he was joined by the Czech valet with the vacant stare. He too clearly wanted to avoid the rest; he made sure he was not being followed before he went to talk to the Russian.

Polyxena strained her ears to hear what they were whispering to each other, but she could not understand a word, in spite of the deathly silence all around.

Then the light was turned off in the servants' hall and the gravel path disappeared abruptly, swallowed up in the darkness.

"The Dalibor Tower", she suddenly heard the Russian say.

She held her breath.

There! Again. This time there could be no doubt, "The Dalibor Tower!" She had heard it quite clearly.

So it was something to do with Ottokar, after all? She deduced that the two of them intended to go to the tower, even at this late hour, and were planning something that they wanted to keep from the others.

But the tower had been closed for hours, what could they be going to do? Break into the warden's cottage? Ridiculous idea. Ottokar's foster-parents were as poor as church mice. Or did they plan to attack Ottokar? For revenge, perhaps? She rejected that idea as being at least equally absurd. What could Ottokar have done to them? He never associated with that kind of person at all, hardly even spoke to them.

'No, it must be something deeper.' She felt it so clearly that she was certain she was right.

The gate was quietly closed and she heard the steps of the two men slowly disappearing down the street.

It only took her a moment to make up her mind. 'Stay here and ... and go to sleep? No, no, no. I must follow them.'

She had to be as quick as possible. Any moment the porter might lock the gate and then it would be impossible to get out.

She felt around in the dark for her black lace shawl, she didn't dare relight the candle. 'I don't want to see the faces of those horrible withered corpses again!' She preferred to brave the unknown dangers of the dark, deserted streets. It was not curiosity that drove her out, but the fear of having to stay in the portrait gallery until the morning; the air there suddenly seemed to be musty and stifling, as if it were filled with the breath of ghosts.

When she had slipped through the gate, she paused for a moment to work out which route to take to the Dalibor Tower so as to avoid running into the two men. There was nothing for it but to go the long way round by Spornergasse and across Wallenstein Square. She cautiously crept along in the shadow of the houses, flitting across the streets as quickly as possible.

Outside Fürstenberg Palace there was a group of people chatting. She waited, afraid of being recognised, since she assumed there would be some of the servants among them, and it seemed an eternity before they broke up and went on their way.

Then she raced up the twisting Old Castle Steps, between dark, high stone walls; behind them were trees covered in blossom which caught the moonlight and shimmered in the blackness, filling the air with their overpowering smell.

At every turn of the steps she slowed down and peered into the darkness before she continued up the next flight, so as not to run straight into anyone. She was almost at the top when she suddenly smelt tobacco smoke. 'The Russian!' was the thought that immediately came to mind, and she stopped and stood still, so that the rustling of her clothes would not give her away.

She was wrapped in impenetrable darkness, she could not even see her hand before her eyes. The parapet of the wall to her right reflected the pale gleam of the sickle moon hanging low in the sky and gave off a dull phosphorescent glow, speckled with the shadows of leaves, which shone in her eyes and made it impossible for her to make out even the next step.

She strained her ears, but there was no sound to be heard in the blackness.

Not a leaf stirred.

Sometimes she thought she could hear a soft, suppressed breathing close to her, so close indeed, that it seemed to come from the wall on her left. She stared fixedly into the darkness and, careful not to make the least noise, slowly stretched her head forward – the sound disappeared, and did not return.

'It was probably my own breath, or a bird stirring in its sleep.' She carefully stretched out her foot, so as not to miss the next step, then suddenly a cigarette flared up next to her, illuminating for a second a face that was so terrifyingly close to her own that in another second she would have touched it if she had not jerked her head back with the shock.

Her heart stood still, for a moment it felt as if the ground were giving way under her feet, then she rushed blindly into the night and only stopped when, with trembling knees, she had reached the top of the Castle Steps and by the light of the stars in the clear sky could see the outlines of the buildings and the dull, misty glow of the city at her feet.

Exhausted and almost in a swoon, she leant against the stone pillar of the archway over the side path that led along the top of the slope of the Stag Moat to the Dalibor Tower.

Only now did the face and the figure she had just seen appear before her inner eye in vivid detail. It was a man in dark glasses, he must have been a hunchback, or at least that was how she saw him in her memory, with a long, dark overcoat, red whiskers, no hat, bristly hair like a wig and strangely distended nostrils.

As she got her breath back she gradually calmed down. 'It must have been a poor cripple who just happened to be standing there and who was probably as frightened as I was. It's nothing to worry about.' She looked back down the steps. 'Thank God he's not following me, though.'

In spite of that, her heart went on beating wildly at the shock for quite some time, and she must have spent half an hour sitting on the marble balustrade of the steps recovering from it, until she began to feel cold in the cool night air and the voices of people coming up the steps suddenly reminded her why she was there.

She pulled herself together and tried to shake off the last traces of trepidation, clenching her teeth to control her trembling. The urge to go to the Dalibor Tower once more dominated her and gave her new strength. Was it to find out what the Russian and his companion were doing? Was it to warn Ottokar of a possible danger? She did not even try to decide what her motivation was for following them to the tower. A last few fluttering qualms – perhaps it would be more sensible after all to return home and go to bed – were driven away by her pride in carrying through her plan, even if it did seem pointless, even if it were just for the satisfaction of knowing she had the courage to see it through to the end.

As she climbed the steep slope to the small postern gate above the Stag Moat, she had the silhouette of the dungeon with its pointed cap of stone as a signpost constantly before her eyes. She had the vague idea of going into the Courtyard of Limes and knocking on Ottokar's window, and she was about to enter the ancient walls when she heard hushed voices from below and saw a group of people – presumably the ones who had been coming up the Castle Steps behind her – approaching the foot of the tower through the bushes.

She remembered that a hole had been made in the outside wall of the middle story of the tower, just large enough for someone to crawl through. From the way the sound of whispering gradually subsided, and from the noise of stones being dislodged and falling, she deduced that the people were using it to gain access to the tower.

She quickly jumped over the crumbling steps leading into the courtyard and ran to the warden's cottage where the light from one window gleamed dully behind green cotton curtains. She pressed her ear against the glass and then whispered, as softly as she could,

"Ottokar. Otto-kar."

She listened.

A creaking, barely audible, came from the room, as if someone was stirring in their bed.

"Ottokar?" She tapped the glass gently with her fingernail, "Ottokar?"

"Ottokar?" It was like a whispering echo, "Ottokar, is that you?"

Disappointed, Polyxena was about to slip away, when she heard the toneless voice inside start to speak; it was like someone talking in their sleep. It was a stammering, tortured murmur, interrupted by deep silences and accompanied all the time by a soft rustling, as of a restless hand stroking the counterpane.

Polyxena thought she could make out parts of the Lord's Prayer. The more her ear became accustomed to the silence, the louder the ticking of a pendulum became, and gradually, the more she listened, the more familiar the toneless voice seemed to become.

She could tell that it was the words of some prayer that were being spoken, but she could not make out their meaning, nor for whom the prayer was being said.

As if by magic, the voice aroused vague memories of a kindly old face beneath a white bonnet. "It must be Ottokar's foster-mother, but I've never seen her?"

All at once it was as if a veil in her memory had been torn aside. "Sweet crucified Jesus! By the blood that dripped from Your crown of thorns ..." Once, many years ago, that very same voice had murmured those very same words by her bed! In her mind she could see the wrinkled hands folded in prayer, could see the whole figure as it must be now, in the cottage, helpless and crippled by arthritis. And she knew that it was her old nurse, she remembered the soft touch of her hand on her cheek and the soothing lullabies she had sung her.

Deeply moved, she listened to the halting, weary words that, scarcely audible, came through the gaps round the window.

"O Mother of God, blessed among women, do not let my dream come true, protect Ottokar from the evil threatening him and add his sins to mine." The next part was drowned by the ticking of the clock. "But if it must be, and you will not avert it, then grant that I may be wrong and that the guilt does not lie with her that I love." Polyxena felt the words like a spear piercing her heart. "Release him, O Mother of God, from the power of those who are in the tower planning murder."

After a pause, the voice went on, "Ignore my prayer when in my pain I beseech you to let me die. Fulfil the longing that devours him, but grant that his hands remain free from blood; destroy his life rather than let them be sullied with murder. And if a sacrifice is required, then lengthen my days of pain and shorten his, so that he may not be drawn into evil ... and do not count his longing a sin, I know that he desires it ... for her sake alone. Nor hold it against her; you know that I have loved her from the very first day, as if she were my own child. Grant her, O Mother of God ..."

Polyxena rushed away. She felt intuitively that she would hear words which would tear the picture hanging within her to shreds, and some instinct for self-preservation forced her to flee them. The portrait of her ancestress within her sensed the threat that it might be banished from this living breast and consigned to the walls of Elsenwanger House once more.

In the middle story of the Dalibor Tower, in that grim, circular room where the minions of avenging justice had abandoned their victims to madness and starvation, a group of men were sitting close-packed on the floor around the hole, through which, in days gone by, the bodies of those who had been executed were dropped into the cellar. In the alcoves in the wall were acetylene torches, and their blinding glare sucked all the colour from the faces and clothes of the assembled men; it also smoothed out every nook and cranny, so that everything was divided into bright, bluish snow or harsh, deep-black shadow.

Polyxena had crept into the dark upper room, that she knew from her rendezvous with Ottokar, and was lying flat on her stomach, observing what was going on below through the opening in the floor that connected the two rooms. The men gathered there seemed to be mostly workers from machine-shops or munitions factories, broad-shouldered men with hard faces and even harder fists. Compared with them Ottokar, who was sitting beside the Russian coachman, was so slight he looked like a child. She realised that they were all strangers to him, he did not even know their names.

Aside from the group, squatting on a block of stone, his head sunk down on his chest as if he were asleep, was the actor, Zrcadlo.

It looked as if, prior to her arrival, the Russian had held a speech, for the men were asking him all kinds of questions. There was a pamphlet, from which he might have read, being passed round.

"Peter Alexeyevitch Kropotkin", the Czech valet, who was sitting at his left hand, spelt out the name before he handed it on. "Is that a Russian general? And will we ally ourselves with the Russian soldiers against the Jews when the time comes, Pane Sergei?"

The Russian drew himself up. "Ally ourselves with soldiers? Us? We are going to be the masters! Get rid of the army! Have soldiers ever done anything other than fire on us? We are fighting for freedom and justice and against all tyranny; we are going to destroy the state, the church, the aristocracy, the middle classes; they have ruled us and cheated us for long enough. How often must I tell you, Václav? We must spill the blood of the aristocracy that daily humiliates and oppresses us. Not one single one must be allowed to survive, neither young nor old, nor women, nor children." He raised his fearsome, sledge-hammer fists and foamed at the mouth: his fury was such that he was unable to speak on.

"Yes, blood must flow!" cried the Czech valet, quickly convinced. "We're agreed on that."

There was a mutter of approbation.

"Stop! I don't agree to that!" Ottokar had jumped up and immediately there was a deathly hush. "Attack defenceless women and children? Am I a bloodhound? I protest. I ..."

"Silence! You promised, Vondrejc, you swore an oath!" screamed the Russian and tried to grab his arm.

"I promised nothing, Pane Sergei." Ottokar furiously pushed away the fist that was trying to pull him down. "I swore to reveal nothing of what I see here, even if they were to tear the tongue out of my mouth. And that I will keep. I unlocked the Dalibor Tower for you, so that we can meet here and decide what action to take, but you lied to me, Sergei, you said we would – " but he got no farther, the Russian had finally managed to grab his wrist and pulled him down. There was a short struggle, which was immediately interrupted. A giant of a worker with a broad face stood up menacingly and glared at the Russian. "Hands off him, Pane Sergei! Here anyone can say what they like, d'you understand? I am Stanislav Havlik, the tanner. Blood will flow – good, blood must flow. But there are some people who cannot stand the sight of blood. He's only a musician."

The Russian went pale and the blood drained from his lips. Furious, he chewed at his fingernails, surreptitiously observing the others from beneath his eyebrows, to see what attitude they would take. Discord was the last thing he wanted at the moment; above all, he had to keep the reins firmly in his grasp. He was determined to lead a movement, what banner it went under was unimportant. He had never in his life believed it would be possible to put nihilist theories into practice, he was much too intelligent for that. He left that kind of nonsense to dreamers and fools. But to whip a stupid crowd into a frenzy with anarchist slogans and in the ensuing confusion secure some position of power for himself – to sit for once inside the carriage instead of on the box – that, he realised, was the message behind all the anarchists' teachings. The secret slogan of the anarchists, "You get out of the way and let me in", had long been his, too.

He forced his features into a grin and said, in placatory tones,

"You're right, Pane Havlik, we'll make a thorough job of it by ourselves. We all want the same, after all." He took the pamphlet out of his pocket and read aloud:

"It says here, 'The coming revolution will have a general character, a fact that will distinguish it from all other upheavals. The storm will not affect one country alone, all the countries of Europe will be drawn into it. As in 1848, so today will the impulse that goes out from one country upset all the other countries and fan the flames of revolution throughout Europe.' "

Turning a few pages, he went on, "And then here it says: 'They promised us freedom of labour, the ruling classes, but they turned us into factory slaves, ("But you're not a factory worker, Pane Sergei", came a mocking voice from the back.) they subjected us to our 'masters'. They claimed they would organise industry so that we would have lives fit for human beings, but endless crises and misery have been the result. They promised us peace, but they brought us war without end. All their promises they have broken! ("It's the honest truth, isn't it?" shouted the Czech lackey, full of his own importance, and turned his vacant stare on the rest of the group, looking for the applause which, to his amazement, did not ensue.)

Hear now what His Highness, Prince Peter Kropotkin – my father had the honour of being his personal coachman – goes on to say: 'The state protects exploitation and speculation, the state protects the private property that has been acquired by theft and deceit. The proletarian, whose only fortune is the strength and skill of his hands' " – he lifted up his own muscular arms – " 'can expect nothing from the state; for him it is nothing but an institution which is dedicated to thwarting his freedom at any cost.' And then he goes on. 'Are the ruling classes making progress in practical matters? Far from it. In their blindness they continue to wave their ragged banners, defending selfish individualism, the free competition of man against man, nation against nation, ("Down with the Jews", came a voice from the back.) and the all-pervading power of the centralised state.' And listen to this, 'They swing from protectionism to free trade and

111

from free trade to protectionism, they go from conservatism to liberalism and from liberalism to conservatism, from religious dogmatism to atheism and from atheism to religious dogmatism. ("Woof, woof", shouted some joker at the back, and a few laughed.) Always looking timidly back over their shoulders at the past, their inability to create anything of lasting worth is becoming more and more evident.' And this, 'Anyone who supports the 'state', must also approve of war. The state is – and must be – constantly endeavouring to increase its power; it must be constantly endeavouring to be more powerful than neighbouring states, if it does not want to be a plaything in their hands. That is why war will remain indispensable to the European states. But one or two more wars will give this decrepit machinery the coup de grâce.' "

"That's all well and good", interrupted an old artisan impatiently, "but what should we be doing now?"

"Didn't you hear?" the Czech valet told him in withering tones. "Kill the Jews and the aristocrats! Kill everyone who sets himself up above the rest. We must show them who the real masters are."

The Russian shook his head in desperation and then, as if looking for help, shot a glance at Zrcadlo, who was still sitting dreamily on his stone, not taking part in the argument at all. Once more he drew himself up to make a speech. "What should we be doing now, you ask? I would rather ask you, 'What must happen?' The troops are at the front, there are only women and children left at home, and – and us. What are we waiting for?"

"But there are still the railways and the telegraph", objected Havlik, unperturbed. "If we attack tomorrow, then by the day after tomorrow Prague will be full of machine guns. And then? Goodbye revolution."

"Well if it comes to that, which I don't believe, then we'll show them we know how to die", shouted the Russian. He slapped the pamphlet. "Who will hold back when it's for the good of all mankind? Freedom doesn't come just by wishing, it has to be seized!"

112

"Pánové – gentlemen! Calm and cold-blooded, that's what we must be!" It was the Czech lackey who spoke, with a grandiose rhetorical gesture. "Pánové! There is an old diplomatic saying, 'Money first, money next and money last!' I ask", he rubbed his finger and thumb together, "does Pan Kropotkin have *peníze*, does he have money?"

"He's dead", muttered the Russian.

"Dead?! Oh, well then ..." the valet's face lengthened. "Then all this talk is for nothing."

"We'll have a mint of money!" cried the Russian. "What about the silver statue of St. Nepomuk in the Cathedral that weighs three thousand pounds? Aren't there millions of pearls and diamonds in the Capuchin Monastery? Isn't there treasure hidden in Countess Zahradka's palace with the ancient imperial crown?"

"You can't buy bread with that", came the voice of the tanner. "How can we turn it into money?"

"No problem", chirped the lackey, who was full of himself again. "What is the Council Pawnshop for?"

A hubbub broke out, for and against. Each of the revolutionaries wanted to make his voice heard, only the workers remained calm. When the noise quietened down, one of them stood up and said earnestly, "All this idle talk is nothing to do with us. It is only the voice of man. We want to hear what God has to say to us." He pointed to Zrcadlo. "God must speak to us through his lips. Our forefathers were Hussites and did not ask, 'Why?' when the order came to fight to the death. We will be able to do the same. What we do know is that it cannot go on like this. We stole dynamite and hid it, pound by pound, and now we have enough to blow the Hradschin sky-high. He must tell us what we are to do."

There was a deathly hush as all eyes turned to Zrcadlo. Polyxena leant excitedly over the hole in the ceiling. She saw him stagger to his feet, but he did not say a word, just tugged at his upper lip. Then she noticed that the Russian was clenching his hands, as if he were doing everything in his power to bend the sleepwalker to his will. The word 'aweysha' suddenly came back to her mind, and immediately she realised what the Russian, perhaps without being aware of it himself, was trying to do. He wanted to use Zrcadlo as his instrument.

He seemed to be having some success; Zrcadlo was already moving his lips.

'No, that must not happen!' She had not the least idea of what she should do to make him obedient to her will, she just kept repeating to herself, 'That must not happen.'

She had not really taken in the Russian's anarchist theories, but one thing was clear to her: the mob intended to assert its power over the aristocracy. The blood of her ancestors rose up at the very thought. She instinctively sensed what it was that made these doctrines so intoxicating: the craving of the 'slave' to take the place of his 'master'. That those she took to be the originators of the ideas – Kropotkin or Tolstoy or Michael Bakunin – were innocent of this desire, she did not know; she had always held their names in deepest abhorrence.

'No, no, no. It must not happen. I – I – I will not allow it!' She gritted her teeth in concentration.

Zrcadlo tottered to and fro, as if two opposing but equal forces were fighting for mastery, until a third, invisible power intervened, proving stronger than either of the others. When he finally spoke, it was hesitantly. Polyxena was triumphant, feeling that once more she had won some kind of victory over the Russian. Whatever the sleepwalker should say, she was sure he would not be acting as the Russian's mouthpiece.

Suddenly calm and composed, Zrcadlo climbed up onto his stone as if it were a rostrum. Everyone went quiet.

"Brothers! You want God to speak to you? Every man's mouth can be the mouth of God, if you will only believe that it is. It is faith alone that can bring about this transformation. Anything can become God, if you will but believe that it is God.

And if God should speak to you with His own lips, and you believed the words came from the lips of a man, then God's mouth would have been transformed into a man's.

114

Why will you not believe that your own mouth can be the mouth of God? Why do you not say to yourselves, 'I am God, I am God, I am God'? If you say it and believe, then your faith will come to your aid in that selfsame hour.

As it is, you listen for God's voice where there is no mouth, you look for His hand to intervene where there is no arm. In every hand that holds you back, you see the hand of man; in every mouth that contradicts you, you see the mouth of man. In your own arm you see only a man's arm, in your own mouth a man's mouth, not the hand of God and the mouth of God. How can God reveal Himself to you if you have no faith and do not believe that He is everywhere?

There are many among you who believe that your destiny comes from God, at the same time believing you can master your own destiny. Do you believe, then, that you can master God and still remain men?

It is indeed true that you can master destiny, but only when you realise that you are God, for only God can master destiny.

If you believe that you are but men, different from God and separate from God, then you will not be transformed and destiny will rule over you.

You ask, 'Why did God allow the war to happen?' Ask yourselves why you allowed it to happen. Are you not God?

You ask, 'Why does God not reveal the future to us?' Ask yourselves why you do not believe you are God, for then you would know the future, would create it yourselves; each one of you would create that part that is his to create, and from that part, each of you would be able to see the whole.

But you remain slaves to destiny. Destiny is like a stone that rolls and falls, a stone made of grains of sand stuck together; and you are those grains of sand, and you roll and fall with destiny. And as it rolls and falls, so it changes shape, taking on ever-new forms, according to the eternal laws of nature. For until this moment the great stone of humanity was loosely made up of grains of many different colours and shapes all mingled together. But now it is taking on the shape that each grain has

115

in miniature: it is taking on the form of one gigantic human being.

Only now is mankind being created from spirit and clay. And those who are all mind, sober and rational, will be its head, and those who are all feeling, soft and sensitive and responsive, they will be its heart.

That is the way the peoples of the world will be united: not according to race or nation or language, but according to the temper and temperament of each individual.

Had you believed from the very beginning that you are God, then that is how it would have been from the very beginning. But as you did not, you had to wait for destiny to take up its hammer and chisel – that is war and misery – to sculpt the refractory stone into shape. You hope that God will speak to you out of the mouth of the one you call Zrcadlo, the 'mirror'? Had you believed that he is God and not just His mirror, then God would have revealed to you the full truth of what is to come.

But as you lack faith, then it is only a mirror talking to you and it can only reveal a tiny part of the truth.

You will hear it and still not know what you are to do. You do not even know that you have already heard the few words that are the most valuable part of the secrets a man can bear as long as he remains in this mortal world:

A mess of pottage you shall receive, if you do not demand more."

"How will the war finish? Who will win?" The words burst out of the Czech valet in the middle of all this prophecy. "Will it be the Germans, Pane Zrcadlo? What will the end be?"

"The ... the end?" Zrcadlo slowly turned towards him, uncomprehending; his features went slack and the light disappeared from his eyes. "The end? Fire in London and revolt in India, that ... that is the beginning – of the end."

They all crowded round the medium and bombarded him with questions, but he gave no more answers; he was like an automaton, devoid of all feeling.

The Russian coachman stared into space with a glazed look

in his eyes; the reins, by which he had hoped to guide the revolutionaries, had slipped from his grasp.

The game was over for him. Wherever the madness broke out, there would be no leading role for him, however hungry for power he was. A ghost had taken his seat on the box and was now driving the coach.

The whole scene had taken place under the light of one of the acetylene torches, and by now Polyxena was almost blinded by its searing glare. To regain her vision, she fixed her eyes on the dark, yawning pit around which the crowd was sitting.

The flame had burnt itself onto her retina, and at first all she could see was the after-image against a black background. Then other images gradually appeared, ghostly faces rising from the depths below, rendered visible to the physical eye through exhaustion of the optic nerve, the monstrous phantasms of a spectral Walpurgisnacht.

Polyxena could feel every fibre in her body quivering and twitching with a new, alien excitement. Zrcadlo's words were echoing through her mind and had awoken something of which, until that moment, she had been completely unaware.

The men too were in the grip of a violent frenzy. She could see their distorted faces and wild gesticulations, could hear their shouts, "God has spoken to us." – "He said, I am God."

Ottokar was leaning against the wall, silent, his face and lips pale and his staring eyes fixed on Zrcadlo, who was standing as still as if he were hewn from stone.

Polyxena looked at the dark, yawning gap once more and started: were there not figures rising up from it, clothed in mist, not after-images any more, but ghostly reality? There was Ottokar, a second Ottokar, a shadow from the past in his very image, with a sceptre in its hand! Then came a man with a rusty helmet and a strip of black cloth tied over one eye, like Jan Žižka, the Hussite general; and wearing grey prison dress came her ancestress, Countess Polyxena Lambua, who had gone mad here in this very tower. They mixed with the revolutionaries without being seen by them.

117

Then Ottokar's double fused with its living image; the man with the helmet stepped behind Zrcadlo and disappeared; in place of the black cloth a shadow suddenly appeared across his face and the rusty helmet was transformed into a tangle of hair. The spectre of the dead Countess drifted up to the Russian and took him by the throat, strangling him.

He seemed to be able to feel it, for he was fighting for breath, terror-stricken. Her form gradually dissolved under the searing light of the acetylene flares, but the white fingers remained visible.

Polyxena realised what the figures were attempting to tell her through their dumb-show. She directed the full force of her will-power at Zrcadlo and tried to remember what the Tartar had told her about 'aweysha'.

Almost immediately the somnambulist came back to life. She could hear the sniff as he drew in breath through his nostrils. The men started back when they saw the transformation that was taking place.

Havlik stretched out his arm, pointing at the shadow across Zrcadlo's eye, and screamed, "Jan Žižka! Jan Žižka of Trocnov!"

"Jan Žižka of Trocnov", the apprehensive murmur went from mouth to mouth.

"Jan Žižka of Trocnov!" screeched the Czech lackey, covering his face with his hands. "Lizzie the Czech said he would come!"

"Lizzie the Czech prophesied it", came like an echo from the back of the room.

Zrcadlo stretched out his left hand, as if he were feeling for the head of an invisible man kneeling before him. His eyes stared out blindly into space. "Kde máš svou pleš?" Polyxena heard him murmur, "Monk, where is thy tonsure?"

Then slowly, inch by inch, he raised his fist and suddenly brought it down, as if he were hitting it on an anvil. A shudder of horror went through the crowd, as if he had really done what Žižka did at the time of the Taborites and had smashed a monk's skull with his fist.

Polyxena thought she saw the spectre of a man in a grey habit tumble to the ground. The stories of the Hussite Wars, which she had secretly read as a child, came back into her mind: black Žižka in armour on his white horse, facing his warrior host; glittering scythes and nail-studded flails; trampled fields, burning villages, pillaged monasteries.

In her mind's eye she saw the bloody battle against the 'Adamites' led by the wild Borek Klatovsky: men and women both naked, they attacked the Hussites armed with nothing but stones and knives, throwing themselves on them and sinking their teeth into their throats, until the Hussites had cut them down like mad dogs. The last forty of the naked warriors had been surrounded and roasted alive. – She heard the clash of arms in Prague where chains were drawn across the streets to stop the charge of the berserk Taborites; she heard the screams of terror as the garrison fled the Hradschin, the impact of the stone cannonballs raining down on the castle, the thump of the clubs and the clash of the axes, the whirr of the slings ...

She saw how the curse of the dying Adamites – 'May one-eyed Žižka go blind!' – was fulfilled; she saw the arrow as it winged its way towards his remaining good eye, saw him on a hill, supported on either side by his captains, staring into the night of darkness whilst below in the sunshine the battle raged; she heard him give orders which cut down the enemy hosts like corn before the scythe; she saw his hand send out death like a bolt of black lightning. – And then, and then the most horrible of all: Žižka, dead of the plague and yet still alive, his skin stretched over a drum! Its dreadful barking rattle putting all to flight who hear it.

Jan Žižka of Trocnov, blind and skinned, still rode at the head of his troops, invisible, a ghost on a putrefied horse, and led them from victory to victory. Her hair stood on end at the thought that the spirit of Žižka might have arisen from the dead and entered Zrcadlo's body.

A storm of words was pouring from Zrcadlo's lips, now shrill

119

and commanding, now hoarse and urgent, short, broken sentences racing one after the other and tearing judgment out by the roots. The very sound of each syllable was like a blow from a club. What did they mean? She could not tell, the throb of blood was so loud in her ears, she could only guess what he was saying from the wild fire in the men's eyes, from their clenched fists and the way they cringed when, after dropping to a whisper, the speech suddenly broke out like a hurricane lashing across their souls.

And still she could see the fingers of her ghostly ancestress throttling the Russian coachman.

'The images in my soul have turned into ghosts and are intervening down below', she sensed, and she suddenly realised that now she was free of them and could be her own self for a while.

Ottokar turned his face toward the ceiling, as if he could suddenly feel her presence; his eyes were looking straight into hers. They had the dreamy, shut-off look that she knew so well. 'He cannot see or hear anything', she realised, 'the words spoken through the somnambulist are not meant for him. The prayer of the voice in the Courtyard of Limes is being fulfilled: 'Mother of God, blessed among women, fulfil the longing that devours him, but grant that his hands remain free from blood.'

She was suddenly filled with the certainty of her immeasurable love for Ottokar, like the resounding peal of an organ, a love such as she had never imagined a human heart could feel.

As if the curtain that covers the future had been torn aside for a moment, she saw Ottokar with a sceptre in his hand – the ghost that had coalesced with him had become flesh and blood – and the imperial crown on his head. Now she knew what the longing was with which he was consumed for her sake!

'My love is only a pale reflection of his.' She felt crushed, she was no longer capable of thought.

Zrcadlo's speech was like a distant murmuring on the edge of her consciousness. He was speaking of the long-lost glory of Bohemia and of the radiance of its splendour to come. And then,

"King!" Had he not said 'King'? She saw Ottokar start. He continued to look fixedly at her, but now, as if he suddenly recognised her, he paled and clutched his heart as he tried to stop himself falling.

A deafening hubbub suddenly drowned the speaker, "Jan Žižka! Jan Žižka of Trocnov will lead us!"

But Zrcadlo pointed to Ottokar and roared something at the excited crowd. She could not tell what it was, all she saw was her lover collapse unconscious, and heard her own voice cry out, "Ottokar! Ottokar!"

A host of white eyes suddenly turned up towards her. She drew back, jumped up and ran into someone who must have been standing in the darkness behind her.

'It was the hunchback from the Castle Steps', was the thought that went through her mind as she tore open the door of the tower and flew across the Courtyard of Limes into a sea of mist.

Chapter Seven

Farewell

With rapid strides the day was approaching that was the most important date in Dr. Halberd's calendar: the first of July, the journey to Karlsbad.

Every morning at sunrise the red-waistcoated coachman circled round and round the royal castle until the window was opened and he could shout out his latest piece of good news for the housekeeper to relay to her master: the new harness had been polished till it shone; the new coat of genuine synthetic lacquer coachwork enamel had dried nicely on the carriage; Karlitschek had already been whinnying in his stall ...

Halberd could hardly wait for the day of the departure. There is no city in the world, if one lives there, on which one would so willingly turn one's back as Prague, just as, hardly one has left it, there is no city in the world one would so dearly love to be back in. The retired Physician to the Imperial Household was also a victim of this repulsion and attraction, even though he did not live in Prague itself; on the contrary, he lived on the Hradschin.

His cases were standing around the room, already packed. The previous evening, in a fit of rage, Halberd had consigned all Czech Lizzies young and old, Zrcadlos, Manchus and Green Frogs to the devil and, in a burst of unwonted energy, tossed the articles he needed for his Karlsbad stay out of wardrobes and cupboards and into the gaping mouths of Gladstone bags and portmanteaus – the sight was not unlike a real penguin thrusting fish down its offspring's beak – finally hopping and fluttering over the bulging receptacles, all of which had a tangle of trouser-legs, ties and drawers hanging from their lips, until their resistance was broken and the catches shut with a weary snap.

All that he had kept out was a pair of slippers embroidered

with tiger's heads and posies of forget-me-nots done in blue glass beads, and one nightshirt; before he gave way to his fit of rage, he had carefully tied them with string to the chandelier, to stop them creeping away from his blind fury and disappearing for weeks.

The former he now had on his feet and the latter – a kind of voluminous tent reaching down to his ankles, with gold buttons and, at the back, a clip to hold up the long tails, which otherwise would get in the way whenever he performed certain functions – was draped over his skinny frame. With his night-gown billowing out behind him, he paced impatiently up and down the room.

At least, that was what he thought he was doing.

In fact, he was in bed, sleeping the sleep of the just. True, it was the uneasy sleep the just seem to suffer from before they set off on a journey, but at least he was sleeping – and dreaming.

Dreams were a regular, irritating side-effect of his Karlsbad expedition, he was well acquainted with them. They always started in May, but this year they were particularly unbearable. Earlier in his life he had persisted in noting down everything he dreamed in his diary, imagining it was a way of exorcising them. Eventually he discovered it just made them worse, so that there was nothing for it but to submit to the vexation with what grace he could and look forward to the other eleven months during which, as he knew from experience, he was guaranteed deep and dreamless slumbers. As he tossed and turned, his eye happened to catch sight of the tear-off calendar over his bed, and he was mystified to see that it still announced the 30th April, the date of Walpurgisnacht and all its evil happenings.

"That's dreadful", he mumbled. "Four full weeks still to go until the first of June? And the cases are already packed! What-ever am I going to wear? I can't go down to Schnell's in my nightshirt for lunch." The idea of having to unpack everything was a nightmare. He imagined the cases, which were bursting at the seams, spewing out all his clothes, retching and groaning as if they had taken an emetic. He saw countless neckties of all patterns and colours slithering towards him like snakes; the bootjack, furious at having been locked up for so long, was like a lobster snapping at his heels with its claw; and that pink knitted garment – it was similar to a baby's hat, only it had white, patent-leather straps instead of ribbons – disgusting the things inanimate objects could get up to!

'No!' he decided in his dream. 'The cases stay closed.'

Hoping that perhaps he had misread the date, the dreaming Imperial Physician was putting on his spectacles to check the calendar when the room suddenly turned icy cold and the lenses misted over.

When he took his glasses off, he saw a man standing before him, naked, apart from a leather apron round his loins, dark-skinned, tall, unnaturally slim and on his head a black mitre with glints of gold.

Dr. Halberd knew at once that it was Lucifer, and he was not in the least surprised, for he realised that, deep down inside, it was a visitation he had long since expected.

"You are the man who can grant all wishes?" he asked, giving an involuntary bow. "Can you also – "

"Yes, I am the God to whom mankind dedicates its wishes", interrupted the apparition, pointing to its loincloth. "I am the only one of the gods who girds his loins; all the other gods are sexless. I am the only one who can understand wishes. Anyone who is truly sexless can never know what wishes are. All wishes are rooted deep within our sexuality, even if we do not realise it, and even if the flower – the conscious wish – appears to have nothing to do with sex at all.

I am the only merciful one among the gods. Every wish I hear, I grant on the spot. But the wishes I hear are those which stir within men's souls and which I bring to light. That is the meaning of my name, Luci-fero: 'I bring to the light'.

My ear is deaf to the wishes that come from the lips of walking corpses. That is why the living dead that call themselves men shrink from me in horror. I tear apart the bodies of men mercilessly, if their *spirit* desires it; I am like a merciful surgeon, who recognises gangrenous tissue and mercilessly cuts it out.

There are many men whose lips scream for death whilst their spirit screams for life: those I compel to live. Many yearn for wealth, but their spirit longs for poverty, so that they may go through the eye of the needle, and them I make beggars upon earth. Your spirit, and those of your ancestors, longed for sleep in earthly life: that is why I made you physicians to the body, and set your bodies in a stone city and surrounded you with people of stone.

Halberd! Halberd! I know what you want! You long to be young again. But you doubt my power and think I cannot bring back the past; you lose heart and would slip back into sleep. No, Halberd! I will not allow you to. For your spirit also beseeches me: 'Make me young again.'

Therefore I will fulfil *both* your wishes. Eternal youth is eternal future, and in the realm of eternity the past awakes as eternal present."

Halberd noticed that as he spoke these last words the apparition became transparent and that in its stead he could see, where its breast had been, a number becoming clearer and clearer, until all that was left was the date: 30th April.

To put an end to these spectral happenings once and for all, he tried to stretch out his arm to tear off the date, but found that he could not. He realised that he was going to have to put up with 'Walpurgisnacht' and its ghosts a little while longer.

"But I have an enjoyable trip to look forward to', he told himself, 'and a few weeks taking the waters in Karlsbad will do me good and make me a new man again.'

He found it impossible to make himself wake up, there was nothing for it but to sink into deep, dreamless sleep.

The sleepers on the Hradschin had a regular alarm-clock that used to wake them at five every morning: the piercingly shrill sound of an electric tram down in Prague that always made the rails screech as it went round the corner by the Czech Theatre at that particular hour. Halberd was so accustomed to this unpleasant reminder of the 'world' he despised, that he no longer noticed it; but he was disturbed by the inexplicable absence of the screech on this morning. He began to toss and turn as the logical conclusion – 'There must be something wrong down there' – passed through his mind, drawing behind it a whole string of vague memories of what had happened during the last few days.

Quite often – the previous day was the last occasion – he had looked through his telescope, and each time the streets had been crowded with people; the throng had even surged across the bridges, and the unceasing Czech cheers of "Slava!" and "Nazdar!" had reached his windows in the form of a long-drawn-out 'Hahahahaa'. Towards the evening a gigantic poster with a picture of Žižka had appeared, illuminated by hundreds of torches, over the ridge of hills to the north-east of Prague like a white spectre from the underworld. It was the first time since the outbreak of war.

He would not have paid any attention to it had not all kinds of strange rumours already come to his ears: his excited housekeeper had raised all ten fingers as she swore that Žižka had risen from the dead and been seen in the flesh in various places round the town during the night. He knew from long experience that the good citizens of Prague were credulous fanatics for whom nothing was too improbable for them not to keep on repeating it to each other until they believed it themselves and rushed out into the streets to see it, but that such a preposterous idea should find general acceptance was something new.

It was no wonder then that, although he was still half asleep, his mind interpreted the absence of the tram screech as a sign of the outbreak of unrest, and this interpretation was quite correct: on that morning Prague was once again the scene of an uprising.

He was still in bed a few hours later when his *dolce far niente* was interrupted – like Belshazzar's dinner party – by a hand, only this was the hand of his servant, Ladislaus, and did not write on the wall, but gave him a visiting card on which was written:

126

"Walpurgisnacht!" muttered Halberd, convinced for a moment he was still dreaming. "What does the fellow want?" he asked aloud.

"Don't know", was the laconic reply.

"What does he look like?"

"Different every day, if it please your Honour."

"What on earth does that mean?"

"Well, Stefan Brabetz changes his clothes every five minutes. So that no one will know it's him."

Halberd thought for a while. "All right, let him in."

Immediately a throat was vigorously cleared outside the door and, as the servant disappeared, a man scurried into the room on silent rubber soles, managing to squint with both eyes at once, an artificial wart stuck on his nose, his chest covered in tin medals, a straw hat and briefcase clamped under his arm, his hands crossed deferentially. He poured out a torrent of servile words and phrases, concluding with, ".... the honour of presenting my most humble respects to your Royal and Imperial Medical Excellency."

"And what is it you want?" asked the Penguin in a sharp tone, fluttering his hands in irritation beneath the counterpane.

The informer started to let off another barrage of obsequious compliments, but was immediately interrupted.

"I asked what you want!"

"Well, your Ex'llency, if it please your Ex'llency, it concerns the young Countess, sir. A most remarkable young lady, if it please your Ex'llency. Not that I hold it against her! God forbid that I should."

"What Countess?" asked Halberd in astonishment.

"I'm sure now your Ex'llency will know which Countess."

Halberd was silent. His tact prevented him from demanding her name straight out. "Hmm. No. I don't know any Countesses."

"Oh. Well in that case you won't, your Ex'llency."

"Quite right. Hmm. By the way, what has it to do with *me*?"

The private agent perched respectfully on the edge of the chair, like a swallow coming to rest, twisted his hat round in his hands, squinted at the ceiling with a sugary smile, then suddenly burst into a voluble speech:

"You'll excuse the liberty, your Ex'llency, but it's like this: now see, I thought, the young Countess is a beautiful young lady, a fine figure of a girl, as they say ... yes, indeed, and well they might ... Anyway, so I thought to myself, it's a crying shame, I thought, that such a fine lady – and young, too, she could take her pick! – should throw herself away on a scruffy nobody like that Vondrejc, who hasn't got two pennies to rub together. So ... well, I thought, there's that Doctor Halberd, what goes in and out of the house like a ... quite regular, I mean ... and the house would be handy, if you see my meaning, sir, though if the house isn't convenient, I know of a place where every room has its own exit ..."

"How dare you!" exclaimed the Penguin, but then went on in a more conciliatory tone, fascinated to know what would come next, "I would have no use for such a ... such an article."

"If you say so, your Ex'llency", sighed the private agent, disappointment written all over his face. "It was just an idea. Pity though. One word from me to the young Countess – I have something on her, you see, and I thought, one word from me and that Doctor Halberd", Brabetz said pointedly, "won't need to ... er ... go to Lizzie the Czech any more."

It gave Halberd such a shock that for a moment he had no idea what to say.

"You think *that's* why I went to the old hag?! Are you mad!"

The informer raised his hands in horror, "Me think a thing like that? Never entered my mind! Word of honour, your Ex'llency!" He suddenly forgot the squint that was part of his disguise and gave Halberd a calculating look. "Naturally, I'm well aware that your Ex'llency ... had certain ... other reasons than ... sorry! ... other reasons for going to visit Lizzie the Czech. Yes, quite different reasons, and that's why I'm here."

His interest aroused, the Penguin sat up in bed and said, "And those reasons were?"

Brabetz shrugged his shoulders. "I make my living by ... being discreet. I wouldn't go so far as to say that your Ex'llency was directly mixed up in the conspiracy that Lizzie's involved in. On the other hand ..."

"On the other hand what?"

"On the other hand, nowadays you find the most respectable people are suspected of involvement in high treason."

Halberd could hardly believe his ears. "High treason!?"

" 'Suspected of', your Ex'llency, only 'suspected of'. Yeees. Sus-pec-ted." As Halberd clearly did not understand the hint, the agent was forced to be a little more specific. "Only suspected. But unfortunately", he glared at his flat feet, "suspicion is enough. By rights, I ought to have reported this already, it's my duty if any suspicion comes to my knowledge, and I'm a very dutiful person, you can be assured of that, your Ex'llency. Unless of course ... that is unless I should come to the conclusion that the suspicion is unfounded. And then, it's a well-known business principle that if I scratch your back ..." He seemed to be taken by an involuntary itch.

"In other words, you want a br − , a tip?"

"Entirely as you think fit, your Ex'llency?"

"Good." Halberd rang.

Ladislaus appeared.

"Ladislaus, take this creature by the scruff of the neck and throw him down the stairs."

"Very good, Doctor Halberd."

A huge paw was extended, darkening the room, then the next moment informer and servant had disappeared.

Halberd listened. A crash came from the hall below. Then heavy footsteps thundered down the stairs after the living missile. "Goodness me, it looks as if Ladislaus is going to pick the fellow up and throw him down the Castle Steps as well. Such devotion to duty!" muttered Halberd, crossing his arms and closing his eyes to continue his morning daydreams.

Hardly a quarter of an hour had passed before he was startled out of his slumbers by a whining noise.

Immediately the door was cautiously opened and Baron Elsenwanger, followed by Brock, his tan retriever, crept into the room on tiptoe, a warning finger raised to his lips.

"Konstantin! Good to see you. But what brings you here so early in the morning?" shouted the delighted Penguin, but the words froze on his lips when he saw the empty, moronic smile on his friend's face. "Poor devil", he muttered to himself, "he's lost what little brains he had."

"Shh, shh", whispered the Baron mysteriously, "shh, shh. Please don't, please don't." He looked round anxiously, quickly pulled a yellowing envelope out of his pocket and threw it onto the bed. "Take it, Halberd, take it, only, please don't, please don't."

The old retriever put its tail between its legs, fixed its half-blind, milky-white eyes on its demented master and opened its mouth wide as if to howl, but not a sound came from its throat. An uncanny sight.

"What is it you don't want me to do?" asked Halberd sympathetically.

Elsenwanger raised his finger. "Thaddaeus, I beg you. Please don't, please don't. Y'know ... y'know ... y'know", with each whispered word he came closer to Halberd, until his lips were almost touching his ear. "The police are after me, Thaddaeus, and the servants know about it, too. Shh, shh! They've all run off, even Božena."

"What? The servants have run off? Why on earth did they do that? When did they go?"

"This morning. Shh, shh. Please don't, please don't. Someone came to see me yesterday. Had black teeth. And black gloves. And a squint, both eyes. Someone from, you know, from the police."

"What was he called?" asked the Penguin.

"He said he was called Brabetz."

"And what did he want from you?"

"Xenerl's run away, he said. Shh, shh! I know why she's gone. She knows everything. Shh, please don't! He wanted money. If I didn't give him any he was going to tell all, he said."

"I hope you didn't give him any?"

The Baron had another anxious look round. "I told Wenzel to throw him down the stairs."

'Remarkable: mad and he still did the right thing', thought the Penguin.

"Shh! But now Wenzel's gone too. Brabetz has told him everything."

"But Konstantin, just stop and think for a moment. What is there he could have told him?"

Elsenwanger pointed to the yellowing envelope.

Halberd picked it up. It was open and, as was obvious at the first glance, empty. "What am I supposed to do with this, Konstantin?"

"Jesus, Joseph and Mary, don't, please don't!" wailed Baron Elsenwanger.

Halberd stared at him, completely bewildered.

His eyes crazed with fear, Elsenwanger bent down to his ear again and groaned, "Bogumil ... Bogumil ... Bogumil!"

Halberd began to understand. His friend must have found the envelope, probably by pure chance, somewhere in the picture gallery, and had so convinced himself that it came from his dead brother that, together with his confused memories of Zrcadlo, it had sent him out of his mind.

"Y'know, Thaddaeus, p'raps he's disinherited me because I never went to see him in the Týn Church down there. But, Jee-zusandMary Thaddaeus, we can't go down there, to – Prague! Throw it away, Thaddaeus, throw it away! Only, please don't, don't ... I mustn't know what's in it, otherwise I'd be disinherited. Keep it safe, Thaddaeus, keep it safe, only don't, don't look inside it. And write on the back that it belongs to me, for when you die. But keep it well hidden, d'you hear? It's not safe at my place, everyone knows about it. That's why they've gone. Xenerl's gone too."

"What? Your niece?" cried Halberd. "She's gone? Where's she gone?"

"Shh! Gone. 'cause she knows all about it." Elsenwanger kept insisting to Halberd that she was gone 'because she knew all about it'. That was all he could get out of him.

"D'y'know, Thaddaeus, the whole town's on the streets. Everyone knows about it. Yesterday evening Žižka Hill was illuminated because they were looking for the will. And Brock – " he swivelled his eyes conspiratorially towards the retriever, " – he must have noticed something too. Look how frightened he is. And there's a plague of flies broken out at Countess Zahradka's. Everything covered in flies, the whole palace."

"Konstantin, for God's sake, what's all this nonsense?" cried Halberd. "You know there's never been a single fly there at all. It's just her imagination. You shouldn't believe everything you hear."

"As God is my witness", protested the Baron, beating himself across the breast, "I've seen them with my own eyes."

"The flies?"

"Yes. It's black all over."

"With flies?"

"Yes, with flies. But I must go now. Otherwise the police will be on to me. Keep it safe and sound, d'you hear. And if you die, remember, it belongs to me. But don't read it, or I'll be disinherited. Please don't, please don't! And don't tell anyone I was here, either. Goodbye, Halberd, goodbye."

Silently and on tiptoe, the mad Baron left just as he had entered. Tail between its legs, the dog followed after.

The Penguin was filled with an immense bitterness. He put his head in his hands. "Another one that Death has taken while he's still alive. The poor, poor fellow."

He was reminded of Lizzie the Czech and the way she had bemoaned the loss of her youth. 'And what's all this about Polyxena? And the flies? It's odd, Countess Zahradka's spent her whole life trying to get rid of imaginary flies – and now some real ones finally come along. It's almost as if she drew them here herself.' A vague memory surfaced in his mind of a naked man with a mitre on his head who had said something about the fulfilment of unconscious wishes; that would fit in quite well with the flies.

'I must get away', he was suddenly roused by the thought. 'I must get dressed. Where's that woman with my trousers? The best thing would be to leave today. Anything to get away from this awful Prague. You can feel the madness rising from the streets. I must go to Karlsbad, that'll rejuvenate me.'

He rang.

He waited. No one came.

He rang again.

At last! There was a knock at the door.

"Come in."

Horrified, he threw himself back on the pillows and pulled the counterpane up to his chin. Instead of his housekeeper, it was Countess Zahradka standing in the doorway, a leather bag in her hand.

"For goodness sake, Countess, I've only got my nightshirt on!"

"I never imagined you wore riding boots in bed", muttered the old woman, without looking at him.

'It must be one of her days', thought Halberd, and waited to hear what she would say.

She remained silent for a while, staring into space. Then she opened the bag and handed him an ancient pistol. "How do you load a thing like that?"

Halberd looked at the gun and shook his head. "It's a flintlock pistol, Countess. It's almost impossible to load something like that nowadays."

"But I want to!"

"Well, first of all you'd have to pour gunpowder down the barrel, then a bullet and pack it with some paper. And you'd have to put some gunpowder in the pan. When the flint strikes, the spark sets the whole lot off."

"Excellent. Thank you very much." The Countess put the pistol back in her bag.

"But, Countess, you wouldn't be thinking of using the gun, would you? If you're afraid of disturbances, the best thing would be to go to the country."

"You mean I should run away from the scum, Halberd?" The old woman gave a fierce laugh. "That'll be the day! But let's talk of something else."

"And how are you, Countess?" said Halberd hesitantly, after a pause.

"Xena's run off!"

"What!? Run away! Good God, has something happened to her? Aren't they looking for her?"

"Looking for her? Why? Do you think it will be better if they find her, Halberd?"

"But how ever did it come about? Tell me what happened, Countess."

"How it came about? She's been gone since St. John's Eve. Presumably she's living with that Ottokar ... Vond-rejc. I always thought it would happen. The blood, you know. Fellow came to see me recently, long blond beard, green pince-nez. ("Aha, Brabetz!" muttered the Penguin.) Said he knew something about her. Wanted a bribe. Had him thrown down the stairs, of course."

"Did he not give you any details? Countess! Tell me!"

"Fellow said he knew that Ottokar was my illegitimate son."

Halberd was so indignant, he sat up in bed. "He had the insolence?! I'll see that he's dealt with!"

"Don't go sticking your nose in my affairs, Halberd", snapped the Countess. "There are lots of things people say about me. Have you never heard that before?"

"I would have told anyone who dared to say – "

The old woman did not let him finish. "Because my husband, Zahradka, the late Court Chamberlain, disappeared, they say I poisoned him and hid his body in the cellar. Only yesterday night there were three more of them creeping around trying to dig him up. I took my dog-whip to them."

"I think perhaps, Countess, you are taking the matter too personally", interjected the Penguin. "Perhaps I can throw some light on the matter. You see, on the Hradschin there is a legend that there is treasure buried in Morzin Palace, where you are living now. That was probably what they were trying to dig up."

The Countess gave no answer. Her black eyes flickered round the room.

There was a long pause.

"Halberd", she said at last, "Halberd ...?"

"Yes, Countess?"

"Halberd, tell me, do you think it's possible that if a dead body is dug up after many years that ... flies could come ... out of the ground?"

An icy shiver ran down Halberd's spine. "F-f-flies?"

"Yes. Swarms of them."

Halberd forced himself to keep calm. He turned his face towards the wall so that Countess Zahradka could not see the expression of horror on his face.

"Flies would only come from a fresh corpse, Countess. A human body rots away in only a few weeks if it's in the earth", he said, tonelessly.

The Countess thought for a few minutes, without moving a

muscle, completely frozen.

Then she stood up and went to the door, where she turned round again. "Are you sure of that, Halberd?"

"Quite sure. There is no possibility I am wrong, Countess."

"Good. Adieu, Halberd."

"Au – revoir, Coun-Countess." Halberd just managed to bring the words out.

The sound of the old woman's steps gradually died away in the stone hall. Halberd wiped the sweat from his brow. "The ghosts from my life are coming to say farewell. It's horrible, horrible! All my life I've been surrounded by madmen and criminals, a whole city of them that ate up my youth, and I saw and heard nothing! I was deaf and blind."

He rang the bell in a frenzy. "My trousers! Confound it! Why has no one brought my trousers?"

He jumped out of bed and ran to the banisters in his nightshirt.

Not a sound.

"Ladislaus! La-dis-laauusss!"

Nothing stirred.

"My housekeeper seems to have run off, just like Konstantin's servants. And Ladislaus. The silly ass! I bet he murdered that fellow Brabetz!"

He flung the window open.

Not a soul in the Castle Square.

There was no point in looking through his telescope: there was a flap over the end and he couldn't go out onto the balcony to remove it in his half-naked state.

As far as he could tell with the naked eye, the bridges were swarming with people. "A plague on their silly games! Now there's nothing for it but to unpack all the cases."

He tiptoed over to one of the leather monsters and cautiously opened its jaws, like Androcles with the lion; a flood of collars, shoes, gloves and socks poured over him. But no trousers.

A carpet bag spewed out several crumpled macintoshes larded with brushes and combs, then sank empty to the ground with a weary sigh.

Another seemed to have digested most of its contents, with the help of a reddish fluid that it had extracted from several bottles of mouthwash.

From the belly of an otherwise respectable-looking basket came a ringing sound the moment the Penguin touched it. It was the kitchen alarm-clock which he had packed by mistake and which now, freed from the intimate embrace of a number of pillows and damp towels, warbled its morning song like the lark ascending.

Soon the room looked as if a witches' sabbath had been held in the menswear department of Tietz' Stores. The Penguin was standing on the one remaining island that was free from haberdashery, surveying the volcanic landscape created by the eruption of his fury. His eyes reddened with rage, he peered through the undulating vista to his bed, desperate to get his pocket-watch from the bedside table to see what the time was. He was visited by a sudden urge to bring order to this chaos, and flexed his knees to start the ascent of a glacier of starched shirt-fronts, but just as suddenly his resolve deserted him. Even Captain Scott or Amundsen would have hesitated to brave such obstacles ...

He pondered the problem:

There were only two cases left which might contain the desired item of apparel: either that lanky, yellow rascal from Leipzig – Mädler & Co. – or the massive cube of grey linen over there, like a block of granite carved to form the cornerstone of Solomon's temple.

After considerable hesitation, he plumped for the granite cornerstone, but regretted it immediately. The objects he excavated from it did, it is true, address the needs of the lower half of the body, but not those which were the Penguin's immediate concern. There was a rolled-up, portable rubber bathtub, a pack of tissue paper, a hot-water bottle, and a mysterious container in bronze enamel with a spout, from which a long, red rubber tube emerged to coil itself – a miniature version of Laocoön's

sea-serpents – round the neck of a statuette of Field Marshal
Radetzky, another item which had been packed in error.

A sigh of satisfaction came from Halberd's troubled breast.
Its cause was not, of course, his pleasure at finding the treacher-
ous red tube again, but the realisation that there was now no
further possibility of a mistake: all that separated desire from
fulfilment – the master from his trousers – were the thin sides
of his Saxon valise. Under cover of a mountain of cigar boxes
and brocade waistcoats, his hands extended like a wrestler, the
Penguin crept up on the apparently unsuspecting peace-time
product from the allied kingdom.

Lips tightly shut, a wicked glint in its keyhole and confident
in its own weight and its armour of woven cane, the blond beast
from the banks of the Pleisse awaited the Penguin's attack. The
first wave was a tentative groping, an almost tender pressing and
kneading of all protuberances, then came an irritated tugging of
its brass nose, kicks and finally (presumably intended as
psychological warfare) appeals to the Prince of Darkness, but
all in vain.

This scion of Mädler & Co. was not even susceptible to feelings of pity. It was completely unmoved by the fact that, in the
heat of combat, Halberd trod on the train of his nightshirt: the
heart-rending screech with which the linen tore produced no
response whatsoever. The Penguin ripped off one of its leather
ears and threw it, with a hiss of fury, at the mocking grin on the
mirrored wardrobe.

In vain. The Saxon kept its lips tight shut. A master of
defence, Antwerp was child's play by comparison. For the
blond beast was well aware that the key to overcoming its
defences was a real key, a small metal one, which was safer than
if it had fallen into a gap between the floorboards, a key which
was in a place where the Penguin would not find it in days of
searching: it was on a blue ribbon round Halberd's neck.

Trouserless and wringing his hands, the Penguin towered up
from his island in the sea of desolation, casting despairing
glances round the room, now at the bell on his bedside table, and

138

now down at his own skinny calves from which, bereft of their linen cover, the grey hairs stood out like wires.

Had he been able to find a towel amid the jumble on the floor, he would certainly have thrown it in.

"If only I'd got married", he moaned in a senile whine, "everything would have been different. Now I have to spend the evening of my years abandoned and alone. There is not a single object I possess that speaks to me of love. And is it surprising? I have nothing that was given to me by a loving hand, how should love come from inanimate objects? I've had to buy everything myself, even these things on my feet."

He gave the tiger's-head slippers with their ring of forget-me-nots a melancholy nod. "I bought the most tasteless ones I could find so that I could make myself believe they were a present. I thought they would give the room a homely touch. How wrong I was!" He pictured in his mind the lonely winter's night when, in a fit of sentimentality, he had given himself his own Christmas present.

"God, if only I had a dog at least, that would show me some affection, like Elsenwanger's Brock!" He sensed that he was giving way to the childishness of old age and tried to resist, but found he no longer had the strength. Even his old trick for such moods – to address himself as 'your Excellency' – did not work.

"Oh dear, Zrcadlo was quite right in the Green Frog. I'm a penguin and I can't fly, never could fly."

Chapter Eight

The Journey to Pisek

Someone was knocking at the door, again and again, louder then softer, but Halberd no longer had the courage to call, 'Come in'. He refused to allow himself to hope it might be his house-keeper with his trousers. He could not bear another disappointment! As so often happens to old men and young children, he was wallowing in self-pity. Finally he managed to murmur, "Come in".

Again his hopes were dashed. When he ventured a glance, whose head should he see popping round the door but Lizzie the Czech's.

'That really is the limit!' was what Halberd wanted to say, but he could not even manage to look like 'your Excellency' let alone sound like one. He felt so helpless and abandoned that he would really have liked to beg her to find his trousers for him.

The old woman could tell from his expression how he felt, and it gave her the confidence to edge farther into the room. "Forgive me, Thaddaeus, but I swear no one has seen me. I would never have come to see you here in the Castle, but I must speak to you. Listen to me please, Thaddaeus, just for one minute. It's a matter of life and death, Thaddaeus, and I'm sure no one will come. I waited two hours downstairs until I was sure there was no one left in the Castle. And if anyone should come, I would throw myself out of the window rather than have them find me in your bedroom." She spoke with mounting excitement, becoming more and more breathless all the time.

For a moment the Penguin was caught in two minds between pity and his accustomed concern for the spotless reputation of the name of Halberd which the family had maintained for over a hundred years. Then an almost alien feeling of pride in his own independence welled up within him.

'Everywhere I look I see feeble-minded nincompoops, drunken gluttons, faithless servants, wily landlords, blackmailing riffraff and women who have murdered their husbands; why should I not offer the hand of friendship to an outcast who, in spite of the squalor in which she lives, still reveres my memory and kisses my picture?'

He smiled at Lizzie and held out his hand to her.

"Come in and sit down, Lisinko. Make yourself comfortable. Now calm down and don't cry. I'm glad you've come! Really and truly! Things are going to have to change from now on. I'm not going to let you live in squalor and starve any more. What do I care what people think!"

"Halberd! Th-Th-Thad-daeus!" exclaimed the old woman, holding her hands over her ears. "Please don't say things like that, you'll drive me mad. Insanity is stalking the streets, in broad daylight, and everyone's given in to it apart from me. Keep tight hold of your head, Thaddaeus, don't you go mad, please! Don't say things like that to me, Thaddaeus, or I'll go out of my mind too. But I mustn't, it's a matter of life and death. Thaddaeus, you must flee. Now. This very moment." Mouth open, she listened to the noise coming through the window. "Can you hear it? Can you? They're coming! Quick, you must hide. Can you hear the drum? There! And again! It's Žižka, Jan Žižka of Trocnov. Zrcadlo, the fiend! He stabbed himself and then they skinned him. In my house! In my room! He told them to do it to make a drumskin! It was the tanner, Havlik, who did it. He's marching in front of them, beating his drum. All hell's let loose. The gutters are running with blood. Bořivoj is king, Ottokar Bořivoj." She flung her hands out in front of her and stared as if she could see through the walls. "They'll murder you, Thaddaeus. The nobility's all fled. Last night. Did no one remember you? I must save you, Thaddaeus. They're slaughtering everyone connected with the nobility. I saw one of them bend down and drink the blood flowing in the gutter. There! Listen! The soldiers are coming!" Exhausted, she collapsed to the floor.

Halberd lifted her up and laid her on a pile of clothes. The horror of what Lizzie had told him made his hair stand on end. She came to straight away and started wailing again, "The drum made of human skin! Hide, Thaddaeus, you mustn't die!"

He placed his hand on her lips. "Don't talk just now, Lisinko. Do you hear? Do as I say. You know I'm a doctor and I know best. I'll get you some wine and something to eat." He looked round. "God, if only I could find my trousers! You'll feel better in a minute, Lisinko, it was the hunger that made you dizzy."

The old woman pushed him away and forced herself to speak as calmly as possible, clenching her fists with the effort:

"No, Thaddaeus, you're wrong. You think I'm mad, but I'm not. Everything I said is true. Every single word. At the moment they're only down in Wallenstein Square, the people are so frightened they are throwing their furniture into the streets to try and stop them. There are a few decent fellows who are sticking by their masters and trying to resist them by building barricades. Molla Osman, Prince Rohan's Tartar is leading them. But any moment the Hradschin might be blown up, they've mined the whole Castle. I know, the workers told me."

With a kind of professional reflex action, Halberd put his hand on her forehead to see if she was feverish. 'She's put on a clean shawl', he noticed. 'Good Lord, she's even washed her hair.'

She realised he still thought she was ill and, before she went on, she thought for a moment what she could say to convince him she was right:

"Just be quiet and listen to me for a minute, Thaddaeus. I've come here to warn you. You must flee immediately. Somehow. Anyhow. It can only be a matter of hours before they're up here in Castle Square. Their main aim is to plunder the Treasury and the Cathedral. Your life isn't safe a moment longer, do you understand?"

"But Lisinko", objected Halberd, rather badly shaken in spite of himself, "the army will be here in an hour at most. Such things don't happen nowadays, you know that. I admit it might be pretty tough down in the 'world', in Prague, but up here, where

142

the barracks are?"

"Barracks? Yes. Empty ones. I realise the soldiers will come, Thaddaeus, but only tomorrow, perhaps, or the day after tomorrow or even next week, and that will be too late. I'm telling you Thaddaeus, believe me, the Hradschin is standing on dynamite. As soon as the first machine guns appear, the whole lot will go up in the air."

"Perhaps it will; if you say so. But what am I to do?" croaked the Penguin. "As you can see, I haven't any trousers."

"Well, put some on."

"But if I can't find the key?" moaned the Penguin, with a furious glance at the Saxon suitcase. "And that old bat of a housekeeper's disappeared."

"There's a key round your neck, perhaps that's it?"

"A key? Me? Round my neck?" Halberd clutched at his throat, let out an ear-piercing yelp of joy and skipped over the mountain of waistcoats like a young kangaroo.

A few minutes later, beaming like a boy with a new bicycle, he was sitting in jacket, trousers, socks and shoes on the top of the glacier of starched shirts, opposite Lizzie the Czech on a mountain of socks and towels, whilst far below a colourful river of ties wended its way towards the chamber-pot.

The old woman was prey to her unease again. "There's someone going past outside, can't you hear it, Thaddaeus?"

"It will only be Ladislaus", said the Penguin, unconcerned. Since he had his trousers back, fear and indecisiveness were a thing of the past.

"Then I must go, Thaddaeus! What if he should find me here!? Thaddaeus, for goodness sake, don't put it off any longer. Death is at the door. I just wanted to ..." She took a package wrapped in paper out of her bag, but immediately put it back. "No, no, I can't." The tears suddenly started to pour down her cheeks, and she stood up to go over to the window.

Halberd gently drew her back down onto the mountain of clothes. "No, Lisinko, you're not going to leave like that. Dry your eyes and sit still. I've got something to say."

"But Ladislaus might come in any moment! And you must get away. You must! The dynamite ..."

"Calm down, Lisinko. In the first place, you don't need to worry at all whether that idiot Ladislaus is going to come in or not; and in the second place there's no dynamite going to go off. Dynamite! I ask you! Dynamite is just more of that nonsense they dream up in Prague. I don't believe in dynamite. But that's not important. The important thing is that you came here to save me, didn't you? Didn't you just say 'Has no one remembered you, no one bothered about you?' Do you think I'd be such a cad as to be ashamed of you, when you were the only person to think of me? We must think very carefully about what we're going to do next, Lisinko. Do you know what I think?" Halberd was so happy to be out of his nightshirt that he was carried away with what he was saying and did not notice at all that Lizzie had turned ashen-grey, her hands started trembling and she kept opening and closing her mouth, as if she were suffocating. "What I think is that first of all I'll go to Karlsbad and take you somewhere in the country at the same time. I'll leave you some money, of course, you don't need to worry, Lisinko. And then afterwards we'll settle down together in Leitomischl – no, not in Leitomischl, that's on the other side of the Moldau." It occurred to him that to get there he would have to cross at least one bridge. "But perhaps", he delved deep into his school geography, "but perhaps in ... in Pisek. You can lead a quiet life in Pisek, I've been told. Yes, of course, Pisek's the place. By that I mean", he added hastily, so that she would not get the idea he was hinting at a future honeymoon, "that no one knows us there. You can look after the housekeeping and I'll ... I'll keep an eye on my trousers and things like that. You needn't worry that I'll be too much bother; a little coffee in the mornings with two rolls, my goulash for lunch with three salt-sticks to wipe up the gravy and then, in the autumn, plum dumplings – for God's sake! Lisinko! What's the matter? Jesus and Mary!"

With a gargling noise, the old woman had plunged into the stream of ties at his feet and was about to kiss his boots.

In vain he tried to lift her up. "Come on now, Lisinko, don't be silly. What's so – " he too was so overcome with emotion that the words choked in his throat.

"Leave me, let me lie here, Thaddaeus", sobbed the old woman. "And please, d-don't l-look at me, you-you'll make your eyes – dirty – "

"Lis – ", Halberd gulped, but did not manage to get the name out. He cleared his throat, croaking like an old crow with a bad cold. A passage from the Bible occurred to him, but he could not bring himself to speak it for fear of appearing sententious. Anyway, he could not remember it exactly. Eventually he quoted automatically, "... first cast a stone at her."

It was a long time before Lizzie recovered her composure again. Then she stood before him, suddenly transformed.

Secretly he was afraid – quietly afraid, as old people are who have the experience of a whole life behind them – that the feeling of intoxication would be followed by a rather banal hangover, but nothing of the kind happened.

The person standing before him, her hands on his shoulders, was no longer the grotesque old Lizzie the Czech, nor the young Lizzie he had once known. She wasted no words in thanking him for what he had said and what he had offered her, she did not even mention it. Ladislaus knocked, opened the door, froze in amazement and then quietly withdrew – she did not even glance at him.

"Thaddaeus, my dear, good old Thaddaeus. Now I remember why I felt I had to come here; I had forgotten, that's all. I did want to warn you, and to ask you to leave before it was too late, but that wasn't everything. I'll tell you how it all came about. One evening not long ago I dropped that picture of you – you know, the one I keep on the sideboard – as I was going to kiss it. I was so miserable about it I thought I would die. Don't laugh, it's the only token I have left of you. I was so desperate, I ran over to Zrcadlo's room – he wasn't ... wasn't dead then – to get him to help me." She gave a shudder as Zrcadlo's gruesome end came back to mind.

"To help you? What do you mean, to help you?" asked Halberd. "How could Zrcadlo have helped you?"

"I can't explain, Thaddaeus, it's a long, long story. I would say that I would tell you another time if I did not know perfectly well that we will never see each other again; at least not ..." Her face suddenly became radiant, as if suffused with a reflection of the enchanting beauty of her youth. "But no; I will not say it out loud. 'Young whores make old bigots', you might think."

"Was this Zrcadlo a ... a friend of yours? Don't misunderstand me, Lisinko, I meant ..."

Lizzie the Czech smiled. "I know what you mean. There can be no misunderstanding between us any more, Thaddaeus. A friend? He was more than a friend. Sometimes I felt as if the devil himself had taken pity on me in my misery and had entered the body of the actor to bring me relief. Zrcadlo was more than a friend to me, he was a magic mirror in which I could see you whenever I wanted. Just as ... just as you used to be, your face, your voice. How did he do it? I never understood. Miracles can't be explained."

'So passionate was her love for me that my image even appeared to her', thought Halberd to himself, deeply moved.

"I never managed to find out who Zrcadlo really was. One day I found him sitting outside my window in the Stag Moat, that's all I know about him. But, to get back to my story: in my desperation I ran to Zrcadlo's room. It was almost dark there, and he was standing by the wall, as if he were waiting for me. That's how it seemed to me, anyway. I could hardly see him, and when I called out his name, he didn't turn into you as he usually did. I'm not telling a lie, Thaddaeus, I swear it's true: suddenly there was something else there in place of him, something I've never seen before. It wasn't a human being, it was naked, apart from a cloth round its hips, slim-shouldered and with a tall, black thing on its head that glittered in the darkness."

Halberd clutched his forehead, "Strange, very strange, I dreamed of a being like that last night. Did it speak to you?"

"It said something I have only just come to understand. It said,

'Be glad that the picture has been broken. Have you not always wanted the picture to break? I have fulfilled your wish, why do you cry? The picture was a delusion. Be not sad.' And he said more, something about a picture in my breast that can never break; and he talked about a land of eternal youth, but I couldn't really understand him, because I was desperate and kept crying, 'Give me my picture back!' "

"And that was why you felt you had to ...?"

"Yes, that's why I felt drawn to you. Don't look at me, Thaddaeus; it would hurt me if I could see the shadow of a doubt in your eyes. And it sounds such a silly thing for me to say, an old woman and the ... dregs of humanity, but I have always loved you, Thaddaeus. I loved you, and then I loved your picture, but it did not return my love. It didn't answer, not from the heart, I mean. It was always silent, a dead object. And I would so have loved to have been able to believe that I had meant just a little to you, but I couldn't. Whenever I tried to make myself believe it I knew I was lying to myself. And I would have been so happy if I had been able to believe it just once. I loved you in a way you can't imagine. You alone. From the very first moment.

After that I had no peace, day or night, I wanted to come here to ask you for another picture. But every time I set off, I turned back. I couldn't have stood it if you had said 'no'. I saw when you came to visit me how you wanted to take the other one away because you were ashamed to see it on my chest of drawers. Now I have finally plucked up the courage and – "

"Lisinko, as God is my witness, I don't possess a photograph of myself. I haven't had my picture taken since then", the Penguin went on, "but I promise you, as soon as we're in Pisek – "

Lizzie the Czech shook her head. "You couldn't give me such a beautiful picture as you did just now, Thaddaeus. I'll always carry it with me, and it will never be broken. But now, farewell, Thaddaeus."

"Liesel, what are you thinking of – Lisinko!" cried the Penguin clutching at her hand. "You're not going to leave me, now, when we have just found each other?!"

But the old woman was already at the door and waving to him, the tears running down her cheeks.

"Lisinko, for God's sake listen to me!"

The air was rent by a terrible explosion which made the window-panes rattle. Immediately the door was flung open and Ladislaus rushed in, deathly pale. "Vášnosti, your Excellency, they're coming up the Castle Steps. The whole city has been blown up!"

"My hat and ... and my sword", shouted Halberd, "My sword!" Eyes shining, his thin lips pressed tight, he suddenly drew himself up to his enormous height, with such an expression of wild determination on his face that his servant recoiled in astonishment. "My sword! I want my sword, do you understand? I'll show those curs what it means to storm the royal castle. Out of my way!"

Ladislaus blocked the open door. "Your Excellency will not go. I won't allow it!"

"What's that?! Out of my way, I say!" fumed Halberd.

"I won't let your Excellency pass. You can knock me down, if it please your Excellency, but I'm not letting you through." As pale as the whitewashed walls, Ladislaus stood at his post.

"Have you gone mad? Are you in league with them too? Give me my sword!"

"You haven't got a sword, Your Excellency, and there's no point. It's certain death out there. Courage is all very well, but it won't achieve anything. Later on, if you want, I'll take you through the Castle yard to the Archbishop's Palace. From there it'll be easy to escape in the dark. I've barred the heavy oak door, they won't break that down in a hurry! I refuse to let your Excellency throw yourself into the jaws of death."

Halberd calmed down. He looked round. "Where's Lizzie?"

"Gone."

"I must find her. Where did she go?"

"I don't know."

Halberd groaned, all his determination was gone.

"First of all we must get dressed properly", said Ladislaus in soothing tones. "Your Excellency hasn't even put his tie on yet. One thing at a time, more haste, less speed. I'll keep you hidden until the afternoon, by then the worst will be over. For the time being, anyway. Then I'll see if we can find your carriage, I've had a word with Wenzel. He'll wait with Karlitschek by the Strahov Gate after dark. It'll be nice and quiet there. There'll probably be no one at all out there. Right. And now we just need to fix the stud at the back, otherwise our collar will keep riding up. That's it.

Now I'm afraid your Excellency is going to have to have a bit of a wait, but there's nothing else for it. I've worked it all out. And you don't need to worry about later on. I'll tidy up here. They won't murder me, they wouldn't find it that easy and, anyway, I'm Czech myself."

Before Halberd could object to these arrangements, Ladislaus had slipped out of the room and locked the door behind him.

Time, which at other times could rush past so swiftly, now seemed unbearably slow and leaden-footed. As the hours dragged by, the Penguin fell prey to a variety of moods, which swooped down on him then just as swiftly left him, from outbursts of rage, when he hammered on the door with his fists and screamed for Ladislaus, to weary resignation. At times his mind cleared and hunger sent him scurrying to a cupboard where he kept an emergency supply of salami. At others, deep depression at having lost his friend, Elsenwanger, would be followed by an almost youthful conviction he would start a new life in Pisek, only to give way to a realisation of the foolishness of such hopes, which would naturally come to nothing.

Occasionally a quiet satisfaction came over him that Lizzie the Czech had not taken him up on his offer to become his housekeeper, but immediately he felt shame seep through every fibre of his being that so soon after her visit he could dismiss the warmth with which he had spoken to her as mere youthful exuberance.

'I should honour the image of me that she took away in her

breast, instead of dragging it through the mire. A penguin? Me? I'd be happy if I were. It's a swine I am.'

His melancholy mood was only intensified by the sight of the disarray all round him. But even sadness and self-pity could not keep a permanent hold on him. Self-reproach vanished when he thought of the radiance that had transfigured the face of the old woman, and he was carried away by a wordless joy as he pictured to himself the happy days that lay before him in Karlsbad and Pisek.

Before he set out on his 'journey', he once more put on all the 'selves' of which his life had consisted. The 'pedant' was the last outfit he donned.

From time to time the racket and babble of voices outside – now crashing against the foot of the castle like a wild sea, now dying away to a hushed silence as the waves of revolt ebbed – reached his ears, but did not grasp his attention. From his earliest childhood he had felt nothing but contempt, indifference or hatred for the deeds of the mob and everything connected with them.

'First of all, I must shave', he told himself, 'then everything else will follow quite naturally. I can't set out on my journey all covered in stubble.'

As the word 'journey' went through his mind, he felt a slight shock. For a brief second, it seemed as if a dark hand had laid hold of his heart. At the same moment he sensed instinctively that it would be his last journey, but his pleasure at the idea of shaving and then tidying up his room in leisurely fashion dispelled any unease or concern he might have felt.

He was filled with content at the presentiment that the Walpurgisnacht of life was soon to give way to a day more radiant than anything he had experienced during his life; the quiver of assurance that there was nothing he would leave behind on earth of which he need feel ashamed, filled him with joy.

For the first time he truly fulfilled the title of 'Excellency'.

He washed and shaved with meticulous care, filed and polished his nails, folded pair after pair of trousers, put waist-

150

coats and jackets on their hangers and hung them in the wardrobe, arranged his collars in concentric circles and made a magnificent display of his ties. The water was poured away into the bucket, the rubber bathtub rolled up and every boot lovingly stretched over its shoe-tree. Then the empty suitcases were piled one on top of the other and pushed back against the wall. With an earnest face, but not a trace of reproach in his heart, he closed the blond beast from Saxony last of all, and, so that it would never again resist, whoever might rise up against it, he tied the blue ribbon with the key around its muzzle.

Until that point he had given no thought to the costume he should wear on his journey; nor did he need to: the right solution came at the right moment.

In a wall-cupboard papered over with wallpaper was the dress uniform he had not worn for years, beside it his sword and over it his velvet three-cornered hat.

With calm dignity he put it on, item by item – the black trousers with the gold stripes, the shining patent-leather shoes, the coat with its trimming of gold braid and sewn-back skirts, the narrow lace jabot under the waistcoat – buckled on the dress-sword with the mother-of-pearl handle and slipped the chain over his head from which his tortoise-shell lorgnon hung.

He laid his nightshirt on the bed and smoothed down the pillows until there was not a crease to be seen.

Then he sat down at his desk. First he followed Elsenwanger's wishes and scribbled a note on the empty yellowed envelope before taking out his will and appending the following codicil:

"I hereby bequeath all my stocks and shares to Fräulein Liesel Kossut of 7, New World Street, ground floor, Hradschin; if she should predecease me, then they are to go to my servant, Herr Ladislaus Podrouzek, together with all my personal belongings. The one exception is the pair of trousers I wore today; they are hanging from the chandelier: they are to go to my housekeeper.

According to Imperial Domiciliary Regulations, ordinance 47, paragraph 13, the expenses of my funeral are to be borne by the Castle Chamberlain's Office. I have no special wishes as regards the place of burial but, if the Office were willing to approve the cost of conveyance, it would please me very much to be buried in the churchyard at Pisek. However, I hereby specifically make order that *under no circumstances* are my mortal remains to be consigned to the railway or any other mechanical means of transport, nor to be interred in Prague or in any other location across any river."

After he had sealed his last will and testament, Halberd opened the huge pigskin-bound tome and wrote the entries for all the days he had missed. Only in one point did he depart from the habits of his forefathers: when he had finished, he appended his signature and drew a line across the page with his ruler.

He felt that this was appropriate since he had no offspring who might perform the task for him.

That done, he slowly drew on his kid gloves. As he did so, he noticed a tiny package tied up in string on the floor.

"It's probably Liesel's", he muttered to himself. "Of course! She was going to give me something this morning, but then she lost her nerve."

He undid the string and found a handkerchief with the letters L.K. embroidered on it, the very same one that he had remembered so vividly in the Green Frog. He had to force back the rising emotion – 'tears do not go with dress uniform' – but he pressed a long kiss on it. When he slipped it into his breast pocket, he realised that he had forgotten his own handkerchief. "Good old Lisinka, she thinks of everything. I almost set off on my journey without a handkerchief", he whispered to himself.

He found nothing strange in the fact that the very moment he had finished his preparations a key turned in the lock and he was freed from his imprisonment. He was used to everything going like clockwork when he was wearing his dress uniform.

Straight as a ramrod, he walked past Ladislaus and down the steps. His astonished servant gabbled, "Your Excellency, Vášnosti! If you please, there's no danger just now. You can get into your carriage here. They're all in the Cathedral; Vondrejc

is being crowned Ottokar Bořivoj III, Emperor of the World."
As if it were a matter of course that the cab should be waiting
for him at the Inner Castle Gate, Halberd merely replied with a
cool, "I know".

When he recognised the tall slim figure with the calm, aristocratic face in the twilit Castle Courtyard, the coach-driver immediately started adjusting his carriage.

"No, leave the roof down", Halberd ordered, "and drive me
to the New World."

Cabbie and servant were horrified, but neither dared contra-
dict him.

A cry ran along the curving wall as the carriage with the
ghostly grey nag turned into the narrow lane, driving before it
the old people and children gathered there. "The soldiers are
coming! Holy Saint Wenceslas, pray for us!"

Karlitschek stopped outside number seven. By the light of a
dreary lamp Halberd could see a group of women gathered
outside the shack, trying to open the door. Some were bending
down round a dark mass on the ground, others were peering over
their shoulders. They shuffled to one side when Halberd got out
of the cab and approached them. On a stretcher made of four
rough planks lay the lifeless body of Lizzie the Czech, a gaping
wound running from the top of her head down to her neck.

For a moment, Halberd staggered and clutched his heart. He
heard a low voice beside him, "Someone said she tried to stop
them getting through the southern gate of the Castle. They
struck her down."

Halberd knelt down, took the old woman's head in his hands
and looked long and deep into the lifeless eyes. Then he kissed
her on the forehead, stood up and went back to the carriage.

A spasm of horror went through the crowd.

The women silently crossed themselves.

"Where to?" asked the driver.

"Straight ahead", murmured Halberd, "just keep going
straight ahead."

The cab was swaying across damp, misty meadows and soft ploughed fields where the grain was sprouting. The coachman was afraid of the roads: death might come at any moment if anyone should recognise the glittering gold uniform of his Excellency in the open carriage. Again and again he had to drag Karlitschek up by the reins as the horse kept on stumbling and falling to its knees. Suddenly one wheel sank into the mud and the carriage tilted to one side. The driver jumped down.

"It looks like the axle's broke, your Honour."

Halberd gave no answer, but climbed out and started striding on his long legs into the darkness, as if it had nothing to do with him.

"Y'r Ex'llency! Wait a moment! It's not that bad now I look at it. Y'r Ex'llency! Y'r Ex'llency!"

Halberd ignored him. He just kept striding straight ahead.

A slope, a grass-covered embankment: he climbed straight up it.

Low wires that gave off a threatening hum, as if an imperceptible breeze were blowing through them: a railway track ran straight into the dying embers of the setting sun.

Halberd kept going straight ahead, striding from one sleeper to the next. He felt as if he were climbing a never-ending, horizontal ladder. His eyes were fixed on the point in the distance where the rails met. "The place where they meet is eternity", he muttered to himself, "that is the place where everything will be transformed. That must be ... that must be Pisek."

The ground began to tremble, Halberd could clearly feel the sleepers quivering under his feet.

The air was filled with a roaring, as of huge wings.

"They are my own wings", murmured Halberd. "I will be able to fly."

Suddenly a black speck appeared in the distance, at the intersection point of the rails, and grew and grew. A train with no lights was thundering towards him. On either side were tiny red dots, like strings of coral: the fezzes of Bosnian soldiers leaning out of the windows.

"That is the one who can fulfil all wishes. I recognise him. He is coming to meet me!" exclaimed Halberd aloud, gazing at the locomotive. "I thank you, Lord, that you have sent him to me."

The next moment, he was struck by the engine and crushed.

Chapter Nine

Lucifer's Drum

Polyxena found herself in the sacristy of the Chapel of All Saints in the Cathedral. Silent and lost in memories, she did not resist as Božena and another serving woman, whom she did not know, pulled a mouldy, threadbare, musty gown stolen from the treasure-chamber and decorated with tarnished gold, pearls and jewels, over the white spring dress she was wearing. In the light of the tall candles, thick as a man's arm, they secured it with pins and clasps.

The last few days lay behind her like a dream.

She saw them float past: images that were determined to wake for one last time before they fell asleep for ever, shadowy, insubstantial and divorced from any response, as if they belonged to some time that had never existed. Slowly they passed, bathed in a dull, sombre light. As each one disappeared there was a pause before the next, during which the dark-brown grain of the old, worm-eaten sacristy cupboards appeared before her eyes, as if a breath of the present were returning to whisper to her that she was still alive.

In her memory Polyxena could find her way back as far as the moment when she had fled from the Dalibor Tower and wandered through the streets of Prague until her sudden decision to return to the custodian's cottage in the Courtyard of Limes, where she had spent the whole night sitting by Ottokar's bed as he lay unconscious with a palpitating heart, and resolved never to leave her lover again. Everything before that moment – her childhood, the time at the convent, and those years spent among old men and old women, dusty books and all sorts of ash-grey things – seemed lost without trace, as if they had happened to an unfeeling portrait, instead of to her.

From this blackness words began to emerge which were joined by images from the past few days:

Zrcadlo, the actor, is talking, as he had in the Dalibor Tower, but more urgently this time and only to a small group, to the revolutionaries of the 'Taborites', Ottokar and herself. They are in the filthy parlour of an old woman people call Lizzie the Czech. A lamp is smoking. A few men are lounging around, listening to the madman. Again, as in the Dalibor Tower, they believe he has been transformed into the Hussite leader, Jan Žižka.

Ottokar believes it, too.

She alone knows that it is only memories of an old, forgotten legend that come from her mind, acquire shape and enter the mind of the old actor to take on a spectral reality. Without her actively willing it, the magic of aweysha pours out of her, she can neither stop it nor guide it; it seems to act of its own volition, seems to obey other orders than hers; it is born within her breast, that is where it springs from, but another hand holds the reins. She feels that it may be the invisible hand of her ghostly ancestor, Polyxena Lambua.

Then her doubts return; it could be the voice in the Courtyard of Limes praying for the fulfilment of Ottokar's longing that is setting the magic force of aweysha in motion. Her own desires have died away. 'Ottokar should be crowned, as his love desires it for my sake, even if only for a brief hour. What do I care whether I find my happiness through it or not?' It is the last wish that has the strength to raise its whispering voice within her, and even that is probably spoken by her painted likeness rather than by Polyxena herself. Concealed within it like a vampire is the undying seed of the old, bloodthirsty clan of fire-raisers, which has been passed on to her over the generations and which is now using her as a tool in order to partake of the life and fecundity of the impending events. In the gestures and speech of the actor before her she sees how the legend of Žižka, the Hussite general, is gradually being transformed and adapted to the present; a shudder runs through her.

She foresees the end: the ghost of Jan Žižka will lead these crazed men to their deaths.

And in a flurry of images, the magic force of aweysha gives her premonitions physical form, so that Ottokar's longing will be transformed from dream to reality: in Žižka's voice Zrcadlo orders that Ottokar is to be crowned, then he seals his prophecy by giving the tanner, Stanislav Havlik, the task of skinning him and using his skin to make a drum; that done, he thrusts a dagger into his own heart.

Obedient to the command, Havlik bends over the body. Seized with horror, the men flee. She alone cannot; something holds her fast by the door. The likeness within her wants to look on.

At last, at long last, the tanner has finished his bloody task.

Another day appeared before her:

Hours of ecstasy and all-consuming love come and then vanish.

Ottokar is holding her in his arms and telling her of the time that is approaching, a time of happiness, of splendour and glory. He will surround her with all the majesty of the earth; there will be no wish that he will not be able to fulfil for her. Under the ardour of his kisses, her imagination breaks the shackles of impossibility. The hut in the Courtyard of Limes turns into a palace. In his arms she can see the castle that he is building for her rise in the air. He presses her to him, and she feels his blood enter her, feels she will bear his child. And she knows that by that he has made her immortal, that a spiritual ardour will sprout from the heat of coupling, that the body imperishable will rise from her perishable flesh: life eternal that the one gives birth to from the other.

A new image from her memory:

She is surrounded once more by the monstrous figures of rebellion, men with fists of steel, blue jackets and scarlet armbands.

They have formed a bodyguard. After their model, the old Taborites, they call themselves the 'Brothers of Mount Horeb'.

158

They are carrying her and Ottokar through streets decked with red flags that flutter from the houses like swathes of blood.

Beside them and behind them is a howling, raging mob carrying torches and screaming, "Long live Ottokar Bořivoj, Emperor of the World, and his Empress, Polyxena!"

The name Polyxena sounds foreign, as if it does not belong to her; within her she can feel the portrait of her ancestress exulting in the homage she takes as her due.

In the brief moments when the howling subsides the harsh laughter of Havlik's drum can be heard; the tanner has become a human tiger, his teeth bared in ecstatic savagery as he leads the procession.

From side-streets comes the sound of fighting and death; isolated groups, who are still resisting, are being butchered.

She has a vague feeling that all this is happening at the silent command of the painted figure in her breast, and is filled with joy that Ottokar's hands remain unsullied by murder.

He is holding on to the heads of the men who are carrying him, and his face is white. His eyes are closed.

Thus they climb the steps of the Hradschin to the Cathedral.

A cavalcade of madness.

Polyxena woke to full consciousness; instead of the images from her memory, it was the bare sacristy walls that she saw round her once more, and the grain of the old cupboards.

She saw Božena throw herself to her knees and kiss the hem of her gown. She tried to read the expression on her face: there was no trace of jealousy or sorrow, only joy and pride.

With a sound like thunder, the bells sounded out and made the flames of the candles tremble.

Polyxena stepped out into the nave.

At first she was blinded by the darkness, only gradually did the forms of the silver candelabra under the red and yellow lights resolve themselves. Then she could see dark shapes struggling with a figure in white between the pillars and trying to force him to go to the altar – the priest who was to marry them.

She could see him refuse, resist, brandish a crucifix.

Then: a cry, a fall – struck down dead.

Scuffling.

A pause – muttering – a deathly hush.

Then the great door was flung open. The glare of torches filled the Cathedral from outside. The organ flickered in the red glow.

They dragged in a man in a brown monk's habit.

His hair was snow-white.

Polyxena recognised him. It was the monk who stood in the Crypt of St. George every day to explain the black stone sculpture, "The dead woman, who bore a snake instead of a child under her heart."

He, too, was refusing to go to the altar.

Threatening arms reached out towards him.

He screamed and pleaded and pointed to the silver statue of St. John Nepomuk. The arms sank. They listened to him, bargained with him.

Muttering.

Polyxena guessed what it was: he was prepared to marry Ottokar and herself, but not at the altar. She realised he had saved his life; but only for a short space, they will kill him once he has pronounced the blessing. In her mind's eye she saw once more Žižka's terrible fist smashing down on a skull and she could hear his words, "Kde máš svou pleš? Monk, where is thy tonsure?"

This time, she knew, it will be his spectre that guides the fists of the mob.

A pew was dragged in front of the statue and a carpet thrown over the stone slabs. A boy strutted down the aisle, bearing an ivory rod on a purple cushion.

A whisper went through the crowd, "The sceptre of Duke Bořivoj the First!"

It was handed to Ottokar.

He took it as if in a dream and knelt down in his king's robe. Polyxena knelt beside him.

The priest appeared before the statue.

Then a loud voice cried, "Where is the crown?"

The throng became restless and only calmed down when the priest raised his hand.

Polyxena heard his trembling voice speak words of devotion and intercession, such as the Anointed One spoke, and an icy shiver ran down her spine as she remembered that the lips that were speaking them would be silenced forever within that very hour.

The marriage ceremony was over. Jubilation echoed round the cathedral, drowning a faint whimpering. Polyxena did not dare turn round to see; she knew what was happening.

"The crown!" The voice rang out again.

"The crown! The crown!" the cry was taken up from pew to pew.

"It's hidden at Countess Zahradka's", someone shouted. They all thronged to the door, a wild surge.

"To Countess Zahradka's! Countess Zahradka's! The crown! Fetch the royal crown!"

"It's made of gold, with a ruby at the front!" came a screech from the gallery: Božena, who always knew everything.

"Ruby at the front", ran the description from mouth to mouth, and they were all as certain as if they had seen the crown with their own eyes.

A man climbed onto a plinth. Polyxena recognised the lackey with the vacant stare. He threw his arms about and screamed in such a rapacious frenzy that his voice cracked, "The crown is in Wallenstein Palace!"

No one was in doubt any more. "The crown is in Wallenstein Palace!"

Behind the howling mob marched the grim, silent figures of the 'Brothers of Mount Horeb', with Polyxena and Ottokar on their shoulders again, as on the way to the Cathedral. Ottokar was wearing the purple robe of Duke Bořivoj and carrying his

161

ivory sceptre.

The drum was silent.

Polyxena's gorge rose in a surge of hatred for this screaming rabble that could be roused to a frenzy of rape and plunder in a few seconds. 'Lower than wild beasts they are, and more cowardly than the worst cringing cur'; and with a deeply cruel sense of satisfaction, she imagined the end of it all, the inevitable end: the rattle of machine-gun fire and the mountain of corpses.

She glanced at Ottokar and gave a sigh of relief. 'He sees and hears nothing. It is like a dream to him. God grant him a quick death, before he wakes.'

She was completely indifferent to her own fate.

The gate of the Wallenstein Palace was firmly blockaded. The mob attempted to climb the walls, and fell back down with bloody hands: the top was all covered with broken glass and iron spikes.

One of the men brought a huge beam.

Hands grasped it.

Back and forward. Back and forward: the monster charged the obstacle again and again, splintering the oak doors with a dull thud until they were wrenched from the iron hinges and disintegrated.

In the middle of the garden was a horse with a red bridle, glassy eyes, a scarlet blanket on its back and its hooves nailed to a board on wheels.

It was waiting for its master.

Polyxena saw Ottokar bend forward, staring at it, and put his hand to his forehead, as if he were suddenly coming to. One of the Brothers of Mount Horeb went up to the stuffed horse, took the bridle and rolled it out into the street. They lifted Ottokar up onto it, whilst the rest of the horde stormed into the house with blazing torches.

Windows crashed to the pavement, the glass shattering into a thousand fragments; silverware, gilded armour, swords

162

encrusted with precious stones, bronze grandfather clocks were all thrown out and clattered onto the cobbles, piling up into mounds. Not one of the Taborites even looked at them. From inside could be heard a loud tearing noise as they set about the tapestries on the walls with their knives.

"Where is the crown?" Havlik shouted to those in the palace.

"Not here" – roars of laughter – "Countess Zahradka will have it", came the reply amid all the bellowing and braying.

The men lifted the board with the horse onto their shoulders, broke into one of their wild Hussite songs, and set off at a march towards Thungasse, preceded by the bark of the drum.

High above them, his purple robe fluttering in the breeze, sat Ottokar on Wallenstein's charger, as if he were riding over them.

The entrance to Thungasse was blocked by a barricade. A band of ancient servants, led by Molla Osman, welcomed them with a hail of bullets and stones. Polyxena recognised the Tartar's red fez.

To ward away any danger from Ottokar, she involuntarily directed a current of will-power at the defenders; she could feel the aweysha strike among them like a lightning bolt, so that they were seized with panic and fled.

Only Molla Osman was unaffected. He calmly stood his ground, raised his arm, aimed and fired. Struck in the heart, the tanner threw his arms in the air and collapsed.

The yapping of the drum was suddenly silenced.

But immediately – Polyxena's blood froze in her veins – it started up again, more muffled than before, but more blood-curdling, more inflaming; in the air, echoing back from the walls, rising from the ground, it was all around. 'It can't be. It's just the echo. My ears must be playing tricks on me', she told herself and looked for it. The tanner was on his face, his fingers clutching the barricade; the drum had disappeared, but the drum-roll, suddenly turning high and shrill, flew on the wind.

The Taborites swiftly removed the stones and cleared the way. The Tartar kept on shooting, then he threw his revolver away and ran back up the alley into the house of Polyxena's aunt, Countess Zahradka, where all the windows were brightly lit.

With the terrible drum constantly sounding in her ears, Polyxena found herself carried triumphantly forward beside the towering, swaying, dead horse that gave off an overpowering smell of camphor.

High above her sat Ottokar.

In the bewildering glare of the criss-crossing lamps and torches Polyxena was sure she caught sight of a shadowy figure flitting through the crowd, now appearing, now disappearing, now here, now there. It seemed to be naked and wearing a mitre on its head, but she could not make it out clearly. Its arms were moving up and down in front of its chest, as if it were beating an invisible drum. When the procession stopped outside the house, it suddenly appeared at the top end of the street, a shadowy drummer formed from the smoke, and the rattle of the drum seemed to come from a great distance.

'He is naked; his skin has been stretched over the drum. He is the snake that lives within men and sloughs its skin when they die. I ...' Her thoughts were becoming confused. Then she saw the white face of her Aunt Zahradka, distorted with hate, appear over the iron bars of the first-floor balcony, heard her shrill, mocking laugh and her howl of fury, "Off you go, you dogs, off you go!"

The bawling crowd, forcing its way along the street behind them, came nearer and nearer. "The crown! You must give him the crown! You must give your son the crown!" screamed the bedlam of furious voices.

"Her son?!" Polyxena exulted, and she was almost torn apart by a wild, unbridled joy. "Ottokar is of the same blood as I!"

"What? What do they want?" asked the Countess, turning to those behind her in the room. From below Polyxena could see the head of the Tartar, as he nodded and gave some answer, and heard the biting scorn in the old woman's voice, "To be crowned, that's what he wants, is it? Ottokar Vondrejc wants to be crowned? I'll put the crown on his head myself, I will!"

The old woman disappeared into the room. Her shadow appeared on the curtains, bending, as if she were picking something up, and then straightening up again.

Angry hands were hammering on the door below. "Open up! – Fetch that iron bar! – The crown!"

Then Countess Zahradka reappeared on the balcony, her hands behind her back. Ottokar, in the saddle of the stuffed horse carried on the men's shoulders, was almost on the same level as she was, his face only a short distance away from hers.

"Mother! Mother!" Polyxena heard him cry. Then a stream of fire blazed out of the old woman's hand.

"There you have your crown, bastard!"

Shot through the forehead, Ottokar tumbled from the horse.

Still deafened from the dreadful report, Polyxena knelt beside her dead love; she kept on calling his name, and all that she could see was a drop of blood like a ruby on his forehead. She could not comprehend what had happened.

Finally she understood, and knew where she was. But all she saw around her appeared as a tumult of phantasmal images: a raging mob storming the house; a horse on its side with a green board attached to its hooves: a toy blown up to gigantic proportions. And beside it Ottokar's sleeping face! 'He looks like a child dreaming of Christmas', was the thought that occurred to her. 'His face is so calm. That cannot be death? And the sceptre! How happy he will be when he wakes up and finds that he still has it.'

'Why has the drum been silent for so long?' she looked up. 'Of course, the tanner was shot dead.' It all seemed so natural to her: that the red flames were pouring out of the window; that she was sitting on a kind of island, surrounded by a stormy sea of howling people; that the sound of a shot came from inside the house, with just the same strange and earpiercing echo as the previous one; that the mob, gripped with terror, suddenly ebbed, leaving her alone with the dead Ottokar; that the air around her seemed to cry, "The army is coming!"

'There is nothing strange about that, I always knew that was how it had to end.' The only thing that struck her as new and remarkable was the fact that the Tartar could suddenly appear in the middle of the blaze on the balcony and jump down to the ground; that he called to her to follow him, an order that she obeyed without knowing why; that he ran up the alley with his hands in the air to where a line of soldiers wearing the red Bosnian fez was standing, their rifles against their cheeks; that they let him through. Then she heard a sergeant scream to her to throw herself to the ground.

'Throw myself to the ground? Why? Because they are going to shoot? Does the man think I'm afraid they might hit me? I am with child, Ottokar's child. It is innocent, how could they kill it! I am entrusted with the seed of Bořivoj's line, which cannot die, only sleep until it reawakens. I am immune.'

The crack of a salvo sounded close in front of her, so that for a second she lost consciousness, but she continued calmly on her way. Behind her the shouting of the crowd stopped abruptly. The soldiers, standing close beside each other, were like teeth in the jaws of some monster. They still had their rifles pressed against their cheeks. Just one of them moved aside with a jangle of equipment to let her pass through the gap.

She wandered into the empty jaws of the city. She seemed to hear the drumming of the man with the mitre again, soft and muffled, as if from a great distance; it led her on, and she followed past Elsenwanger House; the wrought-iron gate had been torn off its hinges, the garden was a scene of devastation: smouldering furniture, the trees black, the leaves scorched.

She turned her head a fraction. 'Why should I look? Oh, I know why, there is the portrait of ... Polyxena. Now it is dead and can rest in peace.' She looked down at herself and was astonished to see the brocade gown covering her white dress.

Then she remembered. 'Oh yes, we played at 'kings and

queens'! I must take it off quickly, before the drum stops and the pain comes.'

Later she was standing by the wall of Sacré Coeur, pulling the bell. 'That is where I want my picture to hang.'

Halberd's servant, Ladislaus Podrouzek, was standing in the doctor's bedroom, wiping away his tears with the back of his hand. He was so moved, he could not hold them back. "Well I never, his Excellency's put everything away himself so neat and tidy!"

"Poor old hound", he said pityingly, turning to the shivering Brock, who had followed him in and was sniffing round the floor, "have you lost your master as well? You come along wi' me, we'll soon get used to each other's company."

The retriever lifted its muzzle, turned its half-blind eyes towards the bed and howled.

Ladislaus followed its gaze and noticed the calendar. "A good job I saw that. His Excellency'd be furious with himself if he knew he'd forgotten it", and he tore off the out-of-date leaves until the first of July showed. The first date to disappear was that of Walpurgisnacht.

The Angel of the West Window – Gustav Meyrink

Mike Mitchell's translation was awarded The Occult Book of the Year Prize when it was first published in 1992. A complex and ambitious novel which centres on the life of the Elizabethan magus, John Dee, in England, Poland and Prague, as it intertwines past and present, dreams and visions, myth and reality in a world of the occult, culminating in the transmutation of physical reality into a higher spiritual existence.

"The narrator believes he is becoming possessed by the spirit of his ancestor John Dee. The adventures of Dee and his disreputable colleague, an earless rogue called Edmund Kelley, form a rollicking 16th century variant on Butch Cassidy and the Sundance Kid as they con their way across Europe in a flurry of alchemy and conjured spirits. At one point, Kelley even persuades Dee that the success of an occult enterprise depends on his sleeping with Dee's wife. Past, present, and assorted supernatural dimensions become intertwined in this odd and thoroughly diverting tale."
Anne Billson in *The Times*

£12.99 ISBN 978 1 903517 81 9 422p B. Format

Vivo; The Life of Gustav Meyrink – Mike Mitchell

"Mitchell a prolific literary translator, looks at the enigmatic Gustav Meyrink in this vibrant biographical debut. Meyrink, a Prague native, was prominent in the late 1800s through the early 1900s, oddly enough, as a banker, mystic and satirist (best known for *The Golem*). Mitchell scrutinizes the man's odd life and infatuations, especially with the occult, which seems to be at the center of his first marriage's failure. Meyrink is revealed as an eccentric and sensitive individual, taking much of the material for his satire from his own troubling experience with the law, the military and the petit bourgeoisie. In this thorough biography, no angle of Meyrinks' life is left unexamined: his drug use, multiple marriages, and stint in prison (wrongly incarcerated) are discussed in depth. Mitchell's biography is fascinating and extensive, but at times speculative; Mitchell confesses up front to 'a dearth of documentary evidence' and a comparative 'wealth of anecdote... much of it published after his death, and much of it recounting fantastic events.' Still, Mitchell excels at his concise organization and his ability to effectively portray Meyrink through both facts and 'as he appeared to his contemporaries, especially the younger [ones].' This examination of a dark, begrudging and sensational individual makes a for a supremely entertaining biography."
Cevin Bryerman in *Publishers Weekly*

£9.99 ISBN 978 1 903517 69 7 224p B. Format